MW00582315

Night's Nieces

The Legacy of Tanith Lee

Contents

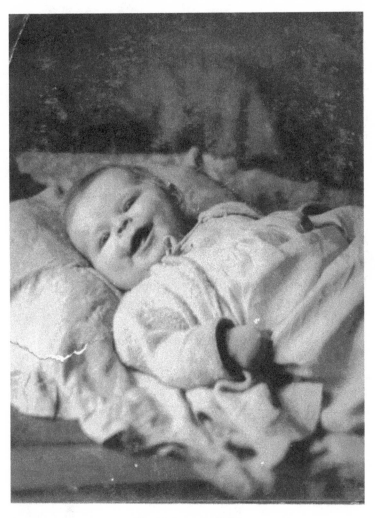

Tanith Lee as a Baby

...and all things are flawless...

John Kaiine

Tanith never wanted children. That would have taken away too much writing time. Though she once said that if she could birth cats, she would: See the story *Tiger I*. Her/our offspring are her novels and tales. It's a big family of one hundred-(ish) books and over three hundred short stories. So when she discovered an interesting, unique female writer, either by chance, recommendation, or a publisher/agent sending an unsolicited MS for a quote, (often delivered way too early in the morning), it was always a thrill for her. As it was when she came upon forgotten writers, such as Malachi Whitaker and Leonora Carrington. She had found silver. She was never one for gold.

I don't remember where we were – some convention, probably Dublin – at the bar with our mate, Harry Harrison, chatting with the committee, when someone asked Tanith if she thought of the 'up and coming' female writers, who had been quoted as saying they had been inspired by her work, as her 'Daughters'. She sipped her wine, thought for a while, and smiled her response: 'No, not Daughters. *Nieces.*' Everyone laughed, but that really stuck with me.

Over the years, her Nieces became very good friends and

groovy company, either in person or on the phone. Cards and emails. There was always creative talks and laughter, and strangely enough vast amounts of booze. Happy memories.

I discussed this collection, (and many other ideas for future anthologies of her work), with Tanith before she died, and she was very happy for me to go ahead with this, and with all of them.

I've found writing this introduction very difficult in many ways. And have been putting it off. Everything I wanted to say has already been said, (almost word for word), in all of the Nieces' individual introductions.

Storm, Sarah, Sam, Cecilia, Vera, Liz, Freda, Kari – Tanith was, and will always be, deeply proud of you all. We both are. Your tribute stories here are beautiful. Thank you. All of our love to you. You will all have your own Nieces. They are reading your words now and being amazed and entranced. Now get back to writing and never, *ever* stop. As you know, Tanith was working – proof reading, which she finished – up until three days before she died. And that was only because she could no longer physically hold a pen.

You are the story tellers, the wise women. Create without wanting or needing to teach. Hold the line. If words run out, invent new languages. If they perish, then paint on the cave walls and concrete towers. From all that you have learnt from her, all of that continuance. *You* are Tanith's Legacy.

The eternal flame of Tanith's words, worlds, characters and images will warm and burn with inspiration into endless new readers, new writers from every continent. New Nieces to come. And hey, probably some Nephews too.

Late November/early December – heavy weather beyond the window. And outside the trees are horizontal from the storm; our Gothic home is shaking. Car alarms all around are going crazy. Johnny Cash is playing way too loud on YouTube. The cats are whowling for yet more food. When I get up to stretch, and look into the gardens, badgers and foxes are cavorting in the first twilight, falling snow. There have been many of Tanith's favourite magpies here today. And (blue) jays, too. The squirrels are well fed. Those of you who really knew her would know that she would love this.

I will organise many more collections of Tanith's stories with various publishers. I am Tanith's estate now and when I'm no longer here, by then, I will have arranged for others to continue her work. She'll be around. **Forever.**

St Leonards on Sea, England
30th November/1st December 2015

Sarah Singleton, Tanith Lee, Storm Constantine
and Liz Williams, 2011

Stained Glass Worlds

Cecilia Dart-Thornton

Yearned I for mountains
glimpsed through stained glass.
Longed I to adventure in the Improbable Beyond.
Thirsted I to drink from the Chalice of Wonder.
Hungered I for nameless fruits from a jewelled tree.
She brought me all, and more!
A word-ship to sail sunset oceans,
A fading horse to bear me through strange skies,
A cup of beauty filled with marvellous draughts,
Blood-red, vinted from bruised cherries
and licentious roses
Spiked with shards of ravening starlight.
She offered goblin fruits –
to taste them is to be enslaved.
Enslaved was I to the magicks of her thought,
A willing thrall to that boundless freedom.

A Spirit of Water

Storm Constantine

When I initially came across Tanith Lee's writing – in my case *The Birthgrave* on its publication in the UK in 1975 – I was captivated from the first page by the author's use of language. I'd not read anything like it before and it spoke beguilingly to my romantic young heart. I'd always invented stories – making them up in my head before I learned to write – and now I had stumbled across a great teacher. Tanith taught me to be brave with words, to break the rules of grammar in some ways, but not in order to mangle the language – to enhance it. She saw the world through clever eyes, fashioning new metaphors, instead of the tired clichés you tended to come across in fantasy at that time (and still do, probably). She taught me how to see reality in a different way, to speak innovatively, to express the language of the spirit.

From discussions with other writers who were – and are – greatly influenced and inspired by Tanith's work, I found that they too had been bewitched by the poetic skill with which Tanith wove words. There is a famous quote from the poet Coleridge: 'Prose: words in their best order; poetry: the best words in the best order.'

Tanith brought this poetic sensibility to the writing of prose.

There are several reasons why I wrote *In Exile* for this collection. First, it involves the sea – an element Tanith loved. I also think she would have liked the story of the bell, (no further spoilers!), which is actually inspired by a true story from Russian history, and also because it's a layered tale – something that Tanith's work taught me about. On the surface, it concerns a young woman somewhat adrift in a strange land and coping with the inexplicable illness of her sister. Second, it explores 'other', and how misconceptions can arise because people misinterpret what is not familiar to them. Thirdly it involves faith, or lack of it. There are things I wanted to say in this piece, without carping, about the conflict of cultures and belief, also about tyranny and that even in the depths of oppression you can be faced with the innocence – or at least unawareness – of those who help perpetrate the oppression because they know no other way. There was a lot going on in my head as I wrote this, and of course it's influenced by what we see around us in the current world.

Tanith's impact on my own work was immense, not least because it encouraged me to write, to overcome the imps of trepidation. Many authors wrestle with a lack of confidence in their wordsmithery and feel they're unable to articulate convincingly the visions and dreams in their heads. The way that Tanith was able to accomplish this so fluently cannot help but be inspiring to other writers. If I'm blocked, reading certain authors – Tanith foremost among them – helps clear the stoppage. It's as if the beautifully-constructed prose flows over me, scouring away mental detritus – the dull preoccupations of mundane life – and makes me love writing again so much I have to get back to it.

Whenever you read one of Tanith's works, you feel it was an effortless endeavour on her part – you can sense how the words must have flowed out of her, not simply like a river, but a succession of splendid cascades, sometimes slowing their course into lazy streams and unfathomable lakes and seas, only once again to surge onwards. The reader is caught by those waters and carried within them, giddy and entranced.

The theme of water – used literally and as a metaphor – crops up continually in Tanith's work. Of all the elements, this is the most represented. She was, I think, part water spirit!

Few writers are of Tanith's calibre, who could write with consistent brilliance. Her love for her work shines from every page, and that is part of her magic. That she had a special gift is indisputable, not only because the quality of her work remained dependably high, but also because she could write without struggle – continually. I have no doubt many writers wish they possessed that gift.

As well as contributing to this anthology, I was also privileged to edit and publish it. Within these pages, you will find stories by nine authors, who were close friends of Tanith, but I'm quite sure there are hundreds of people out there who've been similarly influenced and inspired by her. Since her death, I've heard from other writers who've told me how her work encouraged them to write, helped them overcome their fears and empowered them.

Tanith Lee was taken from this world too early. Even during her final illness, she continued to write – avidly – and still had so much more she wanted to share with us. So many ideas that now will never be written and given life. But her legacy will live on, not just in her published works, but in the hearts and creativity of those whom she inspired. She is with us in the fall of raindrops down a window, in the damp air on the cliffs above a restless sea, in the naiad-haunted tumble of a mountain streams, in the tail of a mermaid shimmering beneath a wave. Like the waters, eternal.

Tanith's Parents, Hylda & Bernard Lee

In Exile

Storm Constantine

Mabelise watched the slave ships come to port. She recognised the flags of *The Curse of the Sea Witch* and *Hasten Home*. Behind them, *Blue Mercy* – slower and smaller. Mabelise heard the crews singing odes to the harbour spirits, their words so ancient no one knew what they meant anymore, which was probably just as well. The ships were empty, of course; their cargo had been sold across the shining sea. Slaves were bred in the temples now, rather than simply taken from them.

The peninsula, as always, shivered with heat, its white rocks blasted and dead, its small trees stringy and parched. The sun, indifferently murderous, desiccated everything. A villa with a turquoise-tiled terrace hung from the side of Seven Eyes Hill. The white, tiered building shimmered, ghostly yet solid, sparkling with quartz. Its terrace was shaded with huge awnings that resembled horizontal sails. The young woman who sat there, curled upon a stone bench in partial shadow, would never be mistaken for a native. Her skin was baked to a reddish brown, her auburn hair bleached in streaks by the relentless sun. Inside the villa, in a pale room, Mabelise's sister Eileenia panted on her bed; the air in this hot land far from home was supposed to help cure her strange malady, which was quite clearly killing her. Their parents had arranged the trip, and a foreign travel agent had accompanied them to this isolated spot, dealing with all official requirements along the way and across borders. Now, they were alone among strangers.

Mabelise was unsure whether the local air was of benefit or not, since she'd noticed no change in her sister's health during the couple of weeks they'd already spent in this cruel country. Perhaps it would take more time. Eileenia's stomach was still intolerant of most foods, her lungs were at best a set of faulty bellows, and her general state that of deteriorating weakness. Mentally, she was disinterested, listless, beyond sadness.

Mabelise was a companion who had no company. Only in the evenings, did Eileenia perk up a little and want to talk, or listen to her sister reading aloud. The rest of the time Mabelise was mostly alone, wandering the house and garden, reading, sometimes attempting to make sketches of the landscape. She had to admit it was liberating not to have to wear stockings and shoes, and to adorn her body with long loose dresses such as the local women wore, but while the slow pace of life, and the fact there were few demands upon her, gave an illusion of freedom, Mabelise felt trapped. How long must they stay here? Until Eileenia recovered or died? What if neither of these things happened and they were stuck here forever, baking and fading away? Generally, the weather made walking and exploring unbearable, this being one of the hottest months of the year, so Mabelise could only be a witness to the land, not a participant. She watched the ships through her spyglass, a gift from her father, and knew their names.

A festival was approaching – old and forbidden, garbed in another name, with different trappings to its past – so the hillsiders were engaged in preparing the land. Pointless to decorate it with flowers, since even if the blooms could be procured they would be swiftly crisped. So the winding lanes, the necklaces of the hills, were dressed with cairns of painted stones. No symbols, but splodges of colour, the most innocent reminder of ages past.

Gazing upon this landscape, the small carefully-placed piles of stones, made Mabelise sad – not an immense feeling, but an acute yet wistful ache, like a star reflected by daylight in the deep water of a well. Grief, she supposed, for a time she'd never known.

Shala, the woman who owned the house where the sisters were staying, stepped out onto the terrace. She was dressed in a cream-coloured robe and head-covering veil, the fabric of which had an ornate border in black and gold thread. A golden ring blistered with pearls pierced her left nostril. Her lips were painted with ochre. Mabelise thought that the skin of the hillsiders was like olives dusted with gold. Never voluble, but always kind, these people had so far kept their secrets. Mabelise knew there were secrets. They were hidden in the stones of the cairns, in the faintly-reflecting sorrow in her heart.

'The girls have made ice peach,' Shala said. 'Come to the kitchen. Take a cup. You're becoming one with the air out here.'

Mabelise realised she could barely move. She felt like a sun-drunk snake, perhaps about to shed her skin. 'The ships have come in,' she said, in a voice that even to her sounded intoxicated.

Shala padded to the edge of the terrace, shaded her eyes to look down upon the harbour. 'The local sailors must be home before the festival,' she said. 'Old beliefs die slow, or not at all.' She turned to Mabelise and smiled. 'Come now, come inside.' This was the first time the invitation had been made; before this Shala had always brought food and drink to Mabelise as if by instinct whenever she felt hungry or thirsty.

The kitchen, at the back of the house and reached by a flight of wide steps, overlooked a sloping garden that was part of the hill. Here, Shala's four girls planted onions and garlic, and tended the bent and wizened trees that nevertheless – Shala insisted – every year became heavy with fruit – peaches, lemons, olives, persea. The girls were not Shala's daughters – she had no man and no children. They did not appear to be staff exactly, but were not quite relatives. They looked so similar they could be sisters, with their pale flowing clothes and thick dark hair that tumbled around their veils. Mabelise had no idea where they'd come from or what their true function was. They weren't very interested in her, even though she was foreign and unknown, but maintained a polite distance. She didn't even know their names, since Shala always addressed them as *fya*, which meant 'loved one'. Sometimes Mabelise heard the girls laughing softly together in some other part of the house. She knew that if she needed them they would be at her side instantly, but other than that she might not exist.

Now, in the dimness of the kitchen, the air cooler than outside and fragrant with peach juice and rose oil, Mabelise was aware of a sense of imminence. Perhaps it oozed from the skins of the girls, from the brightness of their eyes: something about to happen. The girls spoke in whispers, still cutting up fruit at the table, conspiratorial with flashing knives.

'What is the festival about?' Mabelise asked the room in general.

Shala, of course, was the one to answer. 'In the olden times, there was a festival for every day of the year, because a god or a goddess owned each one of them. Ruka Gusa falls over two days, and is the feast of Ruuko and Zalgusa.'

'A god and a goddess?'

'No, two goddesses. Ruuko fashions the flesh of children but cannot give them souls. Zalgusa distils new souls from the matter of the heavens and these are dripped into the mouths of those who will be born. But these are just old stories. No one believes them anymore. Nowadays, people simply see the festivals as a reason to get together and celebrate.'

What Shala did not say, but which Mabelise nonetheless knew, was that the hillsiders were actually proscribed by law from believing in such stories, ever since the Oords had come in their cruel narrow ships, nearly a hundred years before. All of this land, from the peninsula to the sky-piercing mountains of the cold north belonged now to the Oords and their implacable god. His symbol was a lidless eye that could see everything, everywhere and at all times. He had blinded the spirits of Seven Eyes Hill – a story which Mabelise had heard – so perhaps it should now be called Sightless Hill.

'Do you ever wonder what happens to the gods and goddesses people are forced to abandon?' Mabelise asked, her chest fluttery with daring. From the edge of her vision, she noticed the four girls pause at their work for a moment.

Shala raised an eyebrow at her, somewhat stern, then smiled. 'If something isn't real, then it can't have anything happen to it.'

The girls went back to their fruit-cutting, murmuring together, a soothing sound like the insects of evening.

Mabelise wanted to think that Shala and her girls still believed in the old goddesses, even if their devotion was no more than placing a coloured stone beside the road.

That evening, Eileenia felt well enough to sit on the terrace. Shala wheeled her out there in an invalid chair, after having carried her from her bed to the ground floor. Shala was tall and strong, but Eileenia weighed hardly more than feathers anyway. When they'd first arrived, Mabelise had pointed out politely that perhaps Eileenia should have a bedroom on the ground floor, since she could not walk, but Shala had said gently, 'Then she would have no reason to *want* to walk again.'

Shala did not know Eileenia, but perhaps soon she'd realise – as Mabelise had done reluctantly – that Eileenia feigned interest in things to please her sister, that was all.

The evening was warm, and breezes gambolling down the hill brought with them spicy scents of pine and myrrh. A table for dinner was laid beneath the awnings, gentle food of noodles and soft fruits. For Mabelise there was a leg of chicken in a fiery peach sauce. Eileenia couldn't eat meat; it made her stomach hurt too much. One of the girls came out silently into the evening and took a seat at the far side of the terrace. Here she played the *aluud*, a kind of lute, and hummed a wistful tune.

'This could not be more beautiful,' Mabelise said, taking a deep breath of the scented air. She leaned across the table towards her sister. 'How are you feeling, dearest? Is it any better?'

Eileenia shrugged her sharp shoulders and curled a noodle around her fork. This she stared at for a moment before putting it into her mouth, chewed slowly. She did not find joy in food, no matter how fragrant and appetising Shala made it. Mabelise, on the other hand, felt she must have put on far too much weight over the past couple of weeks. She was incapable of refusing any of the delights Shala placed before her.

'I hate being here so much sometimes,' Mabelise said, cutting into her chicken, 'but other times, like now, I wouldn't want to be anywhere else. This land comes alive at night, once the sun stops bullying it.' She frowned. 'I think I'm just lonely. I wish you were better, dearest, and we could go walking.'

'I'm sorry you have to be here,' Eileenia said, and there was no bitterness in her voice. 'I don't think it's doing me any good, anyway.' She raised her head and stared out at the sea.

Mabelise shivered in the balmy air. *She wants to be dead.* The thought came unbidden but sure. 'Don't talk like that,' she said. 'You're certainly not any worse, and that *has* to be good. You have to get better because I refuse to live without you.'

Eileenia smiled a little, shook her head. 'I think it's something you might have to get used to.'

'Stop it, Lina!' Mabelise snapped. 'Remember all the lovely times we've had together. I want them back, and so must you. You have to want it so badly it can't help but happen.'

'I've been ill for less than a year,' Eileenia said in a dull voice, 'but all I can remember is being this way. It

25

was another woman all those good things happened to. They can't come back.'

'Don't give up,' Mabelise insisted, although she knew her words weren't reaching her sister, not really.

At that moment, Shala drifted out onto the terrace, bringing with her a jug of cold milk and a plate of sugared pine nuts.

'There's a moth in your hair,' she said brightly to Eileenia. 'That's good luck.'

And so there was: a small, pale fluttery thing. It folded its wings and remained still on the side of Eileenia's head like a hair ornament.

'How is it lucky?' Mabelise asked.

'Mother Moth brings healing pollen,' Shala said, 'or so our older people say.'

She's used to this, Mabelise thought. Of course, others like Eileenia must have stayed here, because a friend of their mother's had recommended it for invalids. Mabelise wondered how many died and whether any had got well.

Shala placed the milk and nuts on the table. 'Tomorrow evening we'll go down to the port,' she said. 'All of us.'

'For the festival?' Mabelise said. 'I'd love that.' Shala had not offered to take her out before, and she'd been nervous of walking around alone after dark, when it was cool enough to do so.

'I can't do that,' Eileenia said.

'Nonsense,' Mabelise retorted. 'I'll push you in your chair.'

'Your sister is right,' Shala said. 'You are well enough to do this.'

There was something in Shala's tone that made Mabelise think that some words were missing from the end of her speech: *you just don't want to be.* But perhaps that was simply what she thought herself, and she wanted to believe Shala was a knowing ally. So far, the woman had given no indication what she thought of Eileenia's illness or state of mind.

2

Lights filled the village, along with the scent of spiced meat and rose-flavoured sweets. Over the western ocean, the sun descended in a festival display of crimson and orange rays. The masts of the ships were black against the light, the ships as still as phantoms, since all their crews were on land. On the plaza before the harbour, there was a bonfire, and here children danced to the music of the *aluud* and the rhythm of hand drums and finger cymbals. Adults watched indulgently, but did not dance themselves. Within the crowd were the tall blue-white figures of Oord beholders, making sure none of their conquered people ever contravened their rigorous laws.

Mabelise had glimpsed Oords on their journey to the villa, but the travel agent who protected them had been the one to speak to any officials, show them the precious green wafers of permission to travel. Now, as she pushed her sister's invalid chair towards the fire, she saw them; tall creatures almost inhuman, with skin like that of the dead, mottled with blue tattoos that could equally be lines of rot. They either shaved their heads or wound their hair into complicated knots. If there was a Hall of Judgment in the realm of the dead, Mabelise imagined its overseers would look like Oords. She'd yet to see one smile or speak, but that was perhaps because the only ones she'd met had been militia or bureaucrats.

Mabelise's country was not part of the Oordish empire, but even she knew that her leaders treated the Oords very carefully. There was trade between them, and it seemed Oordish ambitions of conquest did not extend to the alliance of lands of which Mabelise and her sister were natives. Possibly, the Oords considered a trade agreement was more convenient than the expense of invasion, in terms of resources and personnel. While they were no direct threat, the Oords were tolerated, appeased even. Mabelise's people could tour freely in Oordish lands, as long as they kept their green wafer travelling permits close to hand; it was considered dangerous not to.

There were stalls set up around the plaza selling sizzled lamb or glazed chicken legs, salads, sweets, fruits and nuts of every type. While strong liquor was frowned upon by the Oords, since lack of personal control was considered the worst of behaviours, a light beverage called *kuana* made of pomegranate, jasmin and other herbal ingredients was permitted – a person would have to drink an awful lot of it to get extremely drunk. This beverage was created solely for festival times; it was light and floral and had the unique gift of, even after a few sips, making you feel as if everything in the world was just fine; it tinted life with gold. Perhaps that was why the Oords allowed it. Shala's girls went to purchase a jug of *kuana*, and returned with a tray also holding seven clay cups. Shala poured out a measure and handed it to Eileenia.

'I can't have liquor,' Eilieenia said.

'Drink this,' Shala said serenely, 'it's mild, and a good medicine for the soul.'

Eileenia took a sip and grimaced, then held the cup in her lap.

Mabelise drained her cup in about four gulps. She'd never tasted anything so *bright* and airy, if a drink could be such a thing. Surely, the ancient goddesses would have drunk it and no doubt gave the recipe to humanity, if not the ingredients themselves.

'You go explore with Jaleya,' Shala said to Mabelise.

One of the girls glanced up, rather startled, from gossiping with her companions, but said nothing.

'I'd rather stay with you,' Mabelise said, 'and Eileenia.'

'It's perfectly safe,' Shala said. 'I'll stay with Eileenia. You should explore. You haven't seen the port yet. You're interested in history, I can tell. There's much of it here.'

Jaleya peeled away from her companions and took Mabelise by the arm. 'Come,' she said.

They walked away from the plaza, up a winding lane. Here there were shops, all shuttered and dark, although lamps burned on the thresholds of the buildings, accompanied by a few painted pebbles. Jaleya didn't converse, but hummed softly, a tune both melancholy and uplifting. Mabelise felt relaxed in the girl's company, as if – through her song – Jaleya was whispering to her like a friend. The doors and windows to the buildings were tall and narrow, the former ornately carved and painted in dusty colours – blue, green, russet. Pots of herbs grew on the window sills, filling the night with bittersweet scent. The port was incredibly ancient and perhaps had not changed for two thousand years. There might have been blood on the streets in the past, but that could be washed away; the buildings, untouched, were eternal.

They came to the top of a hill and here there was a cross-roads. 'I will show you the exile,' Jaleya announced, rather tonelessly.

'Who is that?' Mabelise expected a statue.

'You'll see.' A hint of mischief in Jaleya's voice now.

Ahead of them was a flight of wide, shallow steps, at the top of which was a tall building, much like all the others they had passed, only far bigger. There was a set of double doors in front, high and narrow, and shuttered windows in odd positions, as if they'd been thrown at random at the wall. Jaleya went up to the doors and opened one of them. Mabelise followed her through it. Beyond was a square courtyard with high walls, again studded with dark windows. Steps led to doors on two of the walls. Ornate lamps hung from high sconces, emitting a buttery light. Leafy creepers tumbled down from small iron balconies, and there were flowers – Mabelise could smell them. In the soft lamp-light, blushed with red from the setting sun, she saw them – a host of tiny white stars among the lush leaves.

In the centre of the courtyard was a miniature tower around six feet tall and within it a bell – seemingly too large for its campanile. It was more like a model than anything with real function, the whole structure being so small. There was no room for the bell to swing.

'Here is the exile,' Jaleya said, coming to stand before the shallow steps that surrounded the tower.

'A bell?'

Before Jaleya could speak, an Oord appeared as if from nowhere. Mabelise couldn't help uttering a squeak of shock and grabbed Jaleya's arm again.

'This is Zecksis, beholder of the exile,' Jaleya said, patting Mabelise's clutching hand. 'My friend here is a visitor,' she continued in a louder voice, addressing the Oord, 'I've brought her to see some history. Perhaps you could tell her the story.'

There was a certain tone to Jaleya's voice, which did not indicate fear, submission or hate, as Mabelise might have expected, but humour. Jaleya found the Oord ridiculous, perhaps, yet there was something else. The Oord, Mabelise realised, was young, so perhaps that explained it. He was dressed in a long looping robe that exposed part of his chest. Tendrils of colour crept across his skin, like plants. His head was fairly small and round, covered with knots of hair stiffened with blue-white pigment. His features were also small in comparison to Jaleya's or her own, yet not unattractive. He towered over them.

'Where are you from?' he asked Mabelise in a thick, halting accent.

'Floriland,' she answered and then felt compelled to utter an explanation. 'My sister is very ill. We have come to stay here in the hope the warmth will make her better.'

The Oord nodded. 'Do you know the history of this place?'

Mabelise shrugged awkwardly. 'A little, no great detail.'

Zecksis threw back his shoulders – rather dramatically Mabelise thought – and began to speak. 'In the beginning, when Zamander, our great Darm Lug, sought to bring the word of the Eye to all in this region, he first went to the great city of Askilia, further north along this coast.'

He spoke, Mabelise thought, as if reciting from a script. Clearly, he had learned these words by heart.

'Here, the priests and priestesses of Aska resisted the Word of the Eye, and would not change their ways. They were fighting people and took up arms against

Zamander, who sought to bring only alliance, enlightenment and peace. They were led by the oracle Moora-Tet, who they considered to be an avatar of their high-god. After much needless slaughter, suffering and bloodshed, Moora-Tet was captured and executed. The Askans laid down their arms and peace came to their land. But, as the oracle was flung from the cliffs above the sea, onto the rocks below, one priestess fled to the bell tower of the temple. Alone she pulled the rope of Nilufah, the bell rung only on the shortest day of the year to signify the death of the light. It rang out clear and loud, mourning the passing of Moora-Tet, who had brought only death to his people. Zamander was incensed. He had his soldiers smash down the campanile. He tore out the bell's tongue with his own hands, so it might never speak again. He did not destroy it, but sent it into exile, here, in a courtyard of flowers. He was not a cruel man.'

'What happened to the priestess?' Mabelise couldn't help asking.

'She was no longer part of the story,' Zecksis said, meaning he didn't know, but Mabelise could guess.

Only a mad man would regard the clapper of a bell as a tongue, rip it out, and then send the bell into exile, Mabelise thought. It was not the bell's fault, after all, that it had been rung. And yet the bell had remained in legend, while the priestess was mostly forgotten, just a nameless agent, and here Nilufah was now, silent and dark and motionless. Mabelise shivered. She could almost hear that distant tolling, see the bloodied, weeping woman hanging from the thick rope, pulling with all her strength to let her people know their light had gone out.

'Moora-Tet was said to be very beautiful,' Jaleya said in a coquettish tone. 'The priestess was in love with him, and that was why she rang Nilufah. It was the only way she could express her terrible grief.'

'That is a children's tale,' said Zecksis sternly. 'She rang it out of defiance, and paid for it.'

'And now Nilufah hangs here in her prison, unable to move an inch, forever pondering her dreadful crime,' said Jaleya lightly. 'I hope she is full of regret.'

'She is. You can be sure of it,' Zecksis said, clearly unable to interpret Jaleya's tone.

'There are no bells anymore,' Jaleya said, 'tell my friend why, Zecksis.'

He inclined his head. 'To the Great Eye, the clamour of a bell is dissonance, the voice of debauched gods. The instruments he finds pleasing are the harp and the small flute.'

'Thank you for the story,' Jaleya said. 'It was entertaining, wasn't it, May?'

No one but Eileenia had ever before addressed Mabelise by that nickname. 'Yes,' she answered, 'I feel educated.'

The tall Oord shifted uncomfortably and bowed his head to her. 'Come again,' he said. 'Visitors are always welcome. I can show you the museum inside.'

'Thank you,' Mabelise said. She didn't want to come to this place ever again.

'I will offer prayers for your sister,' Zecksis said.

'You are kind,' Mabelise murmured. She took hold once more of Jaleya's arm.

The two young women returned to the cross-roads and here they stood for a moment staring down at the motionless sea. 'Mother Ocean is so calm among the ships tonight,' Jaleya murmured, 'yet further along the coast, in either direction, she crashes and sprays and mauls the rocks. She would eat all the land.'

'They take slaves from the Temples of Aska, don't they?' Mabelise said abruptly, although she knew the answer.

Jaleya did not flinch, answering firmly, 'Yes. Boys and girls are bred for it there. They are taken across the sea to serve the Eye. It is a reminder that our tongues too could be cut out and silenced at any time.'

'It's dreadful,' Mabelise said inadequately, unable to express the disgust she felt.

Jaleya took her arm. 'Don't grieve for us,' she said, smiling. 'We are the sea.' She sighed. 'Poor Zecksis, you have to feel sorry for him.'

'Do you?' Mabelise said sharply.

'Yes, of course you do. Nilufah's voice might have been silenced, but she can dream and think. I don't think Zecksis can. That's more dreadful, don't you agree?'

'I suppose so.'

There was peaceful quiet for a moment, then Jaleya said, 'Your sister doesn't realise she is free. She traps herself.'

A shiver ran through Mabelise's body. 'Are you talking of death?' she asked, expressing a fear.

'No, no.' Jaleya squeezed the hand that was hooked through her left elbow. 'Come, you've seen the history and it's gone. Let's go back to the others.'

They descended the hill in silence for a while, but before they reached the harbour, the music and the laughter, Mabelise stopped walking and said, 'Is this a dream I'm in? After tonight, will you go back to being one of those mysterious creatures I can't approach, who barely seems to see me?'

Jaleya laughed. 'You had to settle,' she said. 'And we had to be sure you wanted to speak. We heard you and now things are different.'

'Oh...'

'Think on it,' Jaleya said, 'The buildings stand around us, but so much was destroyed. Not a single statue remains, not one inscription. We are all that is left.'

'I understand.' Mabelise looked Jaleya in the eye. 'Like the sea.'

3

In the harbour, they found Shala sitting on the sea wall, legs idly crossed, a clay cup held in one hand in her lap. She was smiling dreamily at the horizon, but came out of her meditation when she sensed Mabelise and Jaleya approach. 'Ah, here you are,' she said. 'I hope you found the tour interesting.'

'Yes, very,' Mabelise said. She looked around for her sister, and then spied with horror the empty invalid chair some feet away. It looked grotesque. 'Where's Eileenia?' she asked. 'Where is she?'

'Hush, no need to worry,' Shala answered. 'My girls took her to shore.'

'She'd never go willingly... She...'

Mabelise ran along the wall, past the quays, until she was above the beach. Here, she peered frantically, but it was too dark to see properly, despite the small fires that had been built on the sand. She climbed over the wall and ran down over the soft, spilling dunes. Had she been separated from her sister on purpose? Had she unwittingly become part of some terrible rite? Ancient gods, passionless sacrifices. A sick woman no one would be surprised to find dead. And few would care; she was a burden, a half life.

Mabelise ran between groups of people gathered round the fires. She ran towards the water, where the sand was damp and shining, the tide far out. She saw four figures, silhouettes against the sky, right at the water's edge. Dizzy, she hurtled on, barely able to breathe. Then she saw Eileenia, supported on either side by two of the girls, ankle deep in the water, holding up her skirt so it wouldn't get wet.

'Eileenia!' Mabelise cried and her sister turned.

She smiled. 'It tickles,' she said, 'when the water runs over my feet. It tickles.'

Incensed Syllables
Discovering Tanith Lee

Cecilia Dart-Thornton

My mother and I shared a love of the same literature. We were both avid readers, and captivated by Sci-Fi and Fantasy. When we children were young, she would faithfully walk with us to the local library every week, my younger sister being wheeled along while seated in an ancient, second-hand 'pusher', my older sister and I skipping alongside. There our mother would borrow books for us. Our parents read to us every evening, before bed.

When we were of school age our mother continued her weekly treks to the library. How we looked forward to the latest batch of books on Library Day, as we tumbled in at the front door after the walk home, our cheeks reddened by summer sun or bitter winter winds! Eagerly we rifled through the treasure trove. Fiercely we debated who would read which title first.

Having no TV in the house, after school we used to play outdoors when the weather permitted, or curl up in an armchair indoors and read the library books.

Mum chose books that were suited to our age group, and some books that were supposed to be for older children. She knew we would try to peruse anything, and wisely allowed us to read beyond our years, if we so wished. Already, I had made a good fist of deciphering most of the 'books for grown-ups' that lined the shelves along the walls of our home. I first read (or rather 'experienced') The Lord of the Rings at the age of nine.

At the same time, our mother – even more wisely – refused to allow us to read anything that might profoundly upset and disturb us, we being empathic and sympathetic children. I quite cheerfully read all the Lang Fairy Books, including their references to people having their heads chopped off or being boiled in oil, but Mum must have known that this stylised, impersonal violence was not meaningful, not upsetting. It was distant – it happened in another time, another place, and was therefore not part of our reality. However, when one day I picked up a woman's magazine Mum had inadvertently left lying about the house and (of course) read it, I was horrified to find a short piece of fiction about a man whose young daughter drowned when the tide came in, despite his frantic efforts to save her. For an impressionable child, it was devastatingly realistic. I ran to Mum in floods of tears.

'I wouldn't have let you read that if I'd known,' she said as she put her arms around me and comforted me.

Because of my parents' wisdom (and the lack of disturbingly violent movies 'for children' in those days) my childhood was largely spent in a world in which it seemed to me that cruelty was so rare it was almost non-existent and truly horrific things hardly ever happened, and when they did they were far away and thus non-threatening. For the empathic child that I was, this was the best possible way to be brought up. It gave me a basic happiness and optimism that laid solid foundations for my world view and without which by now I probably would have perished. When adulthood eventually gave me the mental tools to cope with the Harshness of Life I was able to face the shocking truth and deal with it more easily than if I had been traumatised during my impressionable childhood years.

Thank you, my parents.

To return to literature: I always knew that any book Mum enjoyed, I would enjoy too.

When she discovered *The Birthgrave* at the local library, I must have been in my early teens. She handed me the book – a paperback with a brightly-coloured cover – and said she thought I'd like it.

Like it?

I couldn't put it down.

The sheer beauty of Tanith's language was what first struck me. This was new to me; the use of words to simply to tell a (magnificent, epic) story, but also as poetry in themselves. I was so entranced that I found myself copying out, on odd scraps of paper, some of the lush phrases that had captivated me. Something inside me wanted to keep them, like mementos, in a safe place (my bedroom), to be taken out now and then and gazed at lovingly.

'The smashed green glass of the pool...' I am not sure which of Tanith's books contained this phrase, but it is one of those that riveted teenage me. 'Smashed?' Was one really allowed to write 'smashed' in a published work? I wondered what my Grade 5 teacher would have said about that – she (bless her; she encouraged my literary efforts enormously, in her way) who had crossed out the word 'bit' and substituted in red pen, 'piece' – 'a piece of cloth', in one of my essays. I had gathered, from this, that it was against the rules to write down words that were part of one's everyday vocabulary. A writer was supposed to find words that were more highfalutin'. 'Smash' was a word we would use to describe a car collision or the results of accidentally dropping a glass. Yet Tanith had written 'smashed' – not 'fractured' or 'splintered' or 'shattered'!

By the time I was a teenager I had been writing stories for many years (ever since I first learned to write) – but here, in Tanith's work, was a liberating message; you can use *all* words.

This opened up vast horizons for me.

Not only that, but Tanith's inspiring use of synonyms, similes, metaphors, analogies and startling, unlooked-for adjectives paired with nouns in novel ways – all this was an eye-opener, a joy, a celebration and an education.

I tried to turn the pages of *The Birthgrave* slowly. I tried to savour every well-chosen, incensed syllable; to make the experience linger...

Was it a confluence of factors – my impressionable years, my hard-wired need for flights of fancy and imagination, my hunger for extraordinary stories, the era in which I lived, my past reading experience – was it these elements that, combined with Tanith's genius, gave me one of the most invigorating reading experiences of my life? After my first taste of a Lee story I wanted to try to write the way *she* wrote. For me, there could be no higher style.

But of course I reached the end of *The Birthgrave*, devoured the next two books in the trilogy, and regretted having to turn the final page of the last one. Yet like all the truly good books one reads in one's early years, that first, wondrous reading of *The Birthgrave* stayed with me.

The experience of reading Tanith's fantasy (and I went on to read everything of hers I could lay my hands on, except the horror, for she writes horror so well that it scalds me), will forever influence the way I write.

Like my fellow "Night's Nieces", I made a point of collecting most of Tanith's books, and they occupy a hallowed place on my bookshelves. They are among the few literary works that I often re-read. Tanith enjoyed my "Bitterbynde Trilogy", which was first published in 2001. She was kind enough to write about it; "Dart-Thornton's Bitterbynde trilogy - each book, and all three together, DESERVE TO WIN EVERY FANTASY AWARD THERE IS. This glorious book gives me back my faith in fantasy fiction... a stunning representative of its field... to Cecilia Dart-Thornton I extend the plea: More! More!"

Needless to say, such praise from my idol was far above and beyond all my hopes and expectations. In 2014 I was also honoured to be given the opportunity to publish Tanith's anthology *Phantasya*.

Tanith and I had been corresponding by letter for many years, ever since the mid-1980s, before we finally met in person in England in 2001 and spent a wonderful but far too short day and evening together. We socialised in person again only once after that (due to the tyranny of distance), although we did converse be phone from time to time, and we continued to write to each other right up until the last; I from my home in Australia, she from hers in England. I became a friend of John's too, at those precious, fleeting meetings, and it was John who held me spellbound one evening in May, 2015, as we spoke to each other along the thrumming wires and invisible waves strung across the breadth of the planet; he describing the last hours of Tanith in words of profound love and sorrow, so eloquently that I half-believed I was present, too, at the moment her beautiful spirit flew free at last through the open window.

She will always be with us. Long live the Daughter of the Night.

She that weaves

Words into songs,

Has sent me leaves

Among

The leaves of her letters -

What could be better?

And all her own colours too,

Pale tawny, gold,

Amber and rose,

Perhaps like those

Which drifted with Ophelia...

Fall memorabilia.

Clever Cecilia!

Tanith wrote this poem in response to my sending her, pressed between the pages of a letter, the gloriously-coloured leaves of autumnal liquidambar trees. She loved the leaves and - being Tanith - loved the botanical name of the trees, too.

The Golden and the Dark

Cecilia Dart-Thornton

A shriek ripped through the darkness as a small bird died swiftly beneath a cat's claw. The cat, in its turn, screeched and spat as it was scooped up by a deft hand – a paw? a talon? – and added to the collection in the sack. Or perhaps it was not the cat itself that was stolen, but its cry, its shadow, its fierceness...

Hidden behind dense foliage, a young man watched the squat, diminutive form of the collector as it hobbled through the grey tree-columns with the sack slung over its shoulders – its withers? Its dorsum? Every so often it pounced on novel objects to add to its booty. From between the threads from which the sack was woven, there glimmered a fitful, bluish light, as from eerie marsh-gases.

The watcher pondered. Was this odd-looking wight seeking retribution for the death of woodland animals and birds? But no – there seemed scant connection between the artefacts it chose; a fern leaf here, a scarlet flower there, a pale bone, the unravelling fragment of a spider's web. The young man had never seen the like of this creature – or heard of such a thing, or even dreamed. When first he spied it in the woodland he had thought it one of the trow-folk and concealed himself lest it be offended by his spying; but as it emerged into wan

47

moonlight he perceived it was no trow. There was no protruding snout or lank, bedraggled hair, no glints of silver jewellery; no lopsidedness, or limp.

Stranger than that.

Snails' eyes jutted from the being's large and lugubrious head, and its ears were stiff and ribbed like the wings of bats. Over its shabby garments it wore a dark cloak that was covered with gossamer runes and lettering, as if embroidered in the finest silver thread. Evanescent words seemed to slip and slide and change with every billow of the fabric.

The creature carried also, in one hand, (or paw), a light; an oil lantern, ornate, long-spouted, chased, embossed and filigreed. The flame fluttered spasmodically. By this light it was searching, hunting. It muttered to itself, apparently oblivious of the hidden watcher.

Drawn by curiosity, the young man followed the wight, treading softly in an attempt to remain undetected – though in sooth this molluscan incarnation appeared not one whit wary, or aware of anything outside the scope of its seeking – least of all humankind.

A gust of hysterical laughter swirled like dry leaves from somewhere far off in the woodland. Next, the tragic sobs of a desolate mourner; the heartbroken lament that follows a terrible loss.

Of the joke or the bereavement there was no way of knowing.

Perhaps such jollities or tragedies did not exist. Or perhaps these were but auditory illusions, for the young man knew that the sounds – now replaced by the unintelligible chattering of shrill voices, as in some foreign tongue – were the emanations associated with eldritch wights.

Such beings were rarely glimpsed. He had been fortunate – or unfortunate, time would tell – to have set eyes on the collector-wight at all. This was a rarity. Swift and elusive denizens of the woods, the waters, the hills and the dales were they, the wights, and of certain trees and wells and other haunts where only the brave, the foolhardy, the unwary or the mad among mortalkind would ever dare to venture. Everyone knew well of them by tale and rumour.

Traipsing through uninhabited regions during the sunless hours, the beggar heard the unhuman ones from time to time; their weird, disturbing chittering, their arguments and hysterics, or their rapturous singing, sweet and wild as the song of blackbirds. Their squinting, alien eyes sometimes flashed like ephemeral fireflies from the undergrowth. Sometimes, too, in the secrecy of midnight he witnessed a Faêran Rade go by – a procession of lords and ladies a-horseback, too radiantly beautiful to be of humankind. Then he held his breath, spellbound, in awe at their loveliness, their garments of starlight and smoke, their graceful movements, the jewelled trappings and caparisons of their steeds, whose hoofs never so much as crushed a blade of the whispering grasses... a procession bathed in its own soft glow, like the phosphorescence of sea-foam.

He was, this young man, a prince. Once he had dwelled in an airy castle, whose highest turrets commanded a view for miles around, and all that could be seen from that vantage point belonged to his family. He owned everything he wanted – but that was before the Downfall of the House of Anaturia. His family's enemies had burned down the ancestral seat. Every book in the famous library had been destroyed. Also, and so agonising that it must be thought of last, if at all, they had slain the family and any living thing that might have borne loyalty to the House: the dogs, the horses. The servants. Now, with the bones of his loved ones mouldering beneath the sighing grasses, and the stones of the castle all tumbled down in ruins, and his mind scarred with deep wounds, the young man was no longer a prince. At least, he never dared claim to be.

He was now a beggar.

Ragged and barefoot he ranged the countryside now, petitioning for work or food. His only possessions were a leathern satchel, a water bottle and a knife. He grew accustomed to doors being slammed in his face, dogs being set to harry at his heels, being threatened and driven away. In place of featherbeds with silken counterpanes, straw piles or whispering grasses were his couch; stale crusts he bit in place of delicate viands; instead of harps and songs, harsh words assailed his ears. He craved vengeance, but knew not how to get it.

For fear of the ruthless enemies of the House of Anaturia, no-one, neither aristocrat nor merchant, neither farmer nor serf, would take him in; though many took pity on the young man and gave him food and one day's shelter. Glancing over their shoulders they would urge him to move on; for times were perilous, and spies pervaded the land, which was why he walked at night. None dared hearken to the truth about the betrayal of the House of Anaturia or his discovery of the weak spot in the defences of his enemies... Had they known any of this, would those who sympathised with him have had had the courage to help him fight the injustice?

A youth wandering alone and unguarded – he would long since have fallen prey to bandits and ruffians, only that by chance, when he was a little boy, he had saved a small hedgehog from a noose-trap in a hedgerow, and this furze-pig had turned out to be a fairy, or perhaps the favourite of a fairy (there was no way of knowing). And in return for his good deed he had found himself gifted with a peculiar trait; that, whatever injury anyone tried to inflict on him, it was first inflicted upon the perpetrator. This had resulted in some interesting encounters, from which eventually he had escaped scathe-free. He felt fortunate that his persecutors had not possessed the intellect to deduce the logical circumvention of this enchantment.

When he slept he dreamed of revenge. Dreamed of holding a slim knife, sharpened at the point and bedewed with blood whose colour was indigo, like ink made from the acacia-bush. He drove home the blade, into the hearts of his enemies.

Meanwhile, through the night, the beggar silently followed the snail-eyed wight, until they came to a brook like a ribbon of silver under the moonlight. Bending low, the wight lowered its huge hands like cups into the flow and picked up a handful – not of water but of dripping, twinkling diamonds that flashed a million tiny rainbows. And stowed them in the sack. Next, it reached into the whispering, yellow grasses and tore from them a handful – yet its fist grasped no vegetable blades, only rich hanks of bullion in golden threads. These, too, it crammed into the sack.

A blackbird was singing deep in the woodland, though dawn was still afar-off.

From fragile twigs the wight plucked delicate chains

of cobwebs bedecked with dewdrops. It harvested the smooth, white limbs of birch trees, the downy silkenness of rose petals. Into the sack went all these acquisitions, these *ingredients*, and the watcher wondered why.

To a stone circle they came, the hobbling, snail-eyed thing and its discreet human shadow. In the centre of the ring of monoliths the wight, chanting a song, emptied its sack upon a flat, reclining stone and added the bright, scalding drip of a flame from the lamp.

A meteor tore across the midnight sky, opening it along a blinding seam. With a thunderous roar the very fabric of reality split asunder. Shocked, the young man fell down senseless.

When he opened his eyes, it was dawn. Overhead, clouds pressed upon the lintels of the menhirs and the wind was rising. Beads of chilly dew sparkled blue-white on his threadbare clothes, his clammy skin.

There in the circle's center, upon the stone among the murmuring grasses, sat a woman, golden-haired, clothed in silk and jewels. She was new, amazed and marvelling, beautiful as morning. From her eyes shimmered a silver radiance.

The wight, dimly descried by the cloud-filtered daylight, took her by the hand and led her to a horse, which was waiting nearby. Easily, elegantly, the golden one mounted and rode off. As she departed a white page of paper fluttered down. Handwriting thickly covered it. Before the beggar could catch it to read the words, a sudden gust blew it away.

The collector-wight seemed to melt into the swaying trees and he could no longer find it. Had it *allowed* him to follow it, and now no longer extended that permission?

The beggar-prince jumped up. He could not help but

follow after the woman, and after shouldering his satchel he set off running, but no matter how fast he ran he could not keep up. Nevertheless he stayed on her trail long after it was cold, tracking her through village after village, asking those he encountered along the way, have you seen the woman on horseback? Which way did she go?

Many people replied, 'Yes!' and indicated the direction in which she had travelled. Some gave their answer in tones of joy and exultancy. Others appeared stunned; some were frightened.

Determined not to lose her, the young man plunged beneath the eaves of a mighty forest, far more gloomy, far more ancient and extensive than the dappled woodland in which he had encountered the collector-wight. For countless days and nights he tracked his quarry, until he came to a lonely tower whose damp and moss-covered foundation stones sprouted from a willow-hung riverbank. She was sequestered in the topmost chamber; this he discerned because the barley-sugar light of lamps shone from there. Tilting back his head he spied her through the high window, slightly blurred through the panes, her head bowed. She was writing.

She was no Faêran lady, of this he was certain. She was no wight, either – nor was she quite human. How he knew this, he could not explain.

The tower appeared inaccessible. He supposed it to be enchanted, for he could not find a door. Eventually he gave up trying to gain access and merely waited below, but without any hope.

Next nightfall, pages of writing began to flutter down from the window, one by one, though how they passed through the vitreous panes of those upper fenestrations, the beggar could not understand. He gazed up at the radiant face with the halo of gold hair. She seemed unaware of all except her work; covering pages with words. Her visage was calm, yet exhilarated; she gazed with an abstracted air, as if she perceived unguessed places and things beyond the ken of others. Once more she dipped a quill feather in ink and wrote...

During daytime the window was shuttered and dark, but night after night the lamplight blossomed and she wrote ceaselessly. Pages fountained from the tower's head, showering like shavings of birch-bark.

In the mornings, villagers came paddling up the narrow river in small boats. Wordlessly, eagerly, they gathered the papers and moved away in small groups; reading, reading; gasping, laughing, sighing, exclaiming. Sometimes they held impromptu picnics. Absent-mindedly, kindly, they gave the beggar any spare food. They never came during the dark hours, for fear of eldritch wights.

The young man seated himself on a fallen log beneath the tower, reading any page he could glean. He stuffed them into his satchel to keep them dry. Inside his skull, ruins piled their stones and grew into castles, books rose out of ash and cinders, rubies and lights flashed, windows of coloured glass glared out across fathomless starscapes – the ravaged world within him grew and flourished, bursting into vigour, light, movement, life.

One evening he woke to discover the tower possessed a wooden door. It stood open.

The crowds had gone home, leaving the forest to the plaintive hooting of owls, and the burbling of the river, and the scurryings and gigglings of unseen wights. But standing straight and tall and silent by the tower door was a warrior, strong and muscled, robed in black. A magpie's feather pierced the skeins of his long, coal-coloured mane. Was he her guardian, perhaps? The feather in his hair was both a chieftain's badge of honour and a quill-pen for writing.

The warrior beckoned. Rising to his feet, the beggar obeyed the invitation. The black-haired man moved aside – and there stood she, the Golden One, at the foot of the tower stair. When the beggar stepped up to her and bowed low, she smiled. Her hands reached out, his trembling fingertips touched hers and a thrill flooded him from his soles to the roots of his hair.

Who are you? Why do you write? The beggar intended to ask, but he was unable to force the words past his lips. Such vast numbers of words jostled to be said that he was locked in silence.

Of course he did not love her.

That is, he did love her, but not as a lover would. This was another, more profound bond. The powerful attraction that had caused him to follow her was not *eros*, but some platonic combination of admiration, vision, intellect and idealism.

'The best revenge is to live well', a woman's clear voice uttered, and it startled him because he thought no one had spoken.

'Oh', he said, or thought, or thought he said. 'But what can I do? How can I live well when the world turns me away?'

She smiled again, her eyes brimming with meaning, and nodded as if some message had passed between them, though he did not understand.

Then with a swish of silken skirts the Golden One turned and climbed the stair to the top of the tower. The cloud of her tresses floated at her back. The warrior stepped inside too, and closed the door. He was alone.

The young man ran back to his vantage point, craned his neck and beheld her once more in the topmost room, seated at her desk, dipping a quill feather in ink and commencing to write.

Long he gazed, thanking fate for his good fortune, painfully conscious that such precious moments cannot last.

How long he remained thus, he could not measure. Perhaps for a heartbeat, perhaps for years. As the sky paled the end came – too quickly. He was unprepared.

The light in the tower faded. The oil lamp sputtered out. A final whirlwind of frayed pages blasted out and scattered, spiralling lazily to the ground. From the river a mist began to rise.

The tower door opened, and there they were – the golden woman in the warrior's arms as easily as if she were a child. Her eyes were closed, as if she slept peacefully, yet too pale was she and too still...

The mist shredded, revealing a barge moored at the riverbank. It was draped with sumptuous tapestries and rich velvet the colour of wine. The steersman who waited aboard turned his – its – head; the head of the strange creature with snails' eyes and bat-wing ears. Tenderly the warrior kissed the woman's face, and placed over it a spangled veil. Wading into the water among the tasselled reeds and purple flag-lilies, he laid her gently in the barge. When his task was done he remained standing among the sedges, while all around uprose a weeping, a wailing and a gnashing of teeth, and a yowling of cats.

The steersman pushed off and the vessel floated, smooth and stately away from the widening ripples and nodding rushes, fading into the mist. The warrior climbed from the water and walked away, but he was weeping. A magpie's feather fluttered down from the labyrinths of his dark hair.

The beggar-prince picked it up. The tip of the quill had been sharpened to form a nib, ready to be dipped in ink. Indeed, a few drops of indigo fluid lay trembling inside the shaft.

For an instant he wondered what it was he truly held in his hands – whether the quill of a bird, the quill of a hedgehog or a knife so sharp and slender it could stab his enemies to the heart.

He held the feather carefully. His own tears watered it.

From his leathern satchel he withdrew a leaf of paper, half blank. He smoothed it out, and with the magpie pen wrote one line: 'The True Story of the House of Anaturia.'

It was a beginning...

TO VERA: May 2010

May The Gods
    Guard Your Home
And All
    Therein.

Love always, and thoughts —

(YANITH)

Vera Nazarian

The wonder of Tanith Lee entered my life oh-so-long ago, and shaped me as a writer entirely. In 1976, my parents and I arrived in the United States as refugees from the USSR and the civil war in Lebanon, a month before I turned ten. Immediately I started to learn and devour books in English (my second language after my native Russian). And very soon after, I first came upon Tanith Lee's work.

I vividly remember the paperbacks, in those distinctive DAW editions with the yellow spine. The first was *The Birthgrave*—I believe it was recently published at that point—and there was a marvellous introduction by Marion Zimmer Bradley—whose *Darkover* books I was also consuming at moment, so it doubly impressed me. I started to read—and drowned.

I was transported into impossible antiquity and wonder, with a single book that pressed all my buttons, pulled all my nerves, twisted my senses, fired up my pulse points, and blew my young mind. What was it, precisely? A combination of elegance, beauty, lofty demonic pride, and remote power with an unlimited potential, all contained within a single ivory-towered yet self-effacing female character—a nameless goddess waking in a volcano, with a face of ugliness so terrible it must not be seen (or it must not be ugliness).

Ultimately, the character, that nameless 'she', was a being of perfection and contradictions, and her journey through an exotic ancient world thrilled me on every level. None of that 'she is ordinary human and relatable just like me' nonsense so often touted by the literary establishment as the pinnacle of the kind of characterisation a serious writer must portray—if I wanted 'someone just like me' I could pick up anyone else's mundane books or merely look in the mirror... No, what I wanted was the *other*—a spectacular alien *other* to strike awe into my soul, to terrify me with beauty, to transport me out of my own worthless skin, and make me fly. And Tanith Lee gave me this experience—a chance to know a genuine goddess in the flesh, made real through the power of the author's words. And all of it was written in the most spectacular, extravagant, poetic language I had ever seen. Stunning vivid metaphors rained like blossoms, rich similes danced like mad tongues of flame... My seduction was complete.

The amazing thing is, all of her books were like that— rich, decadent, sublime imagery seething on the page. I began consuming *The Storm Lord* and *The Silver Metal Lover*, *Sabella*, *Cyrion*, *Lycanthia*, *Sung in Shadow*, *Drinking Sapphire Wine*, *Volkhavaar*, all the volumes of *Tales of the Flat Earth*, *Kill the Dead*, *Day by Night*, *Tamastara*, *Days of Grass*, and so on... The books obsessed me, and I searched for them with relentless hunger.

Unlike most other books of fantasy I was reading then, this was true ethereal high fantasy in the loftiest sense, written by an elven goddess or a faerie queen—because she couldn't be a mere human being, I thought. The characters were mythic in nature, archetypal demigods larger than life, perfect in their terrible passions and beauty, loving and hating and desiring on an immortal scale. This was also High Romance—romance in the original definition of novels of medieval chivalry, unrequited courtly love, and dark demonic obsession. I was reading stories of gods and demons often being one and the same, and the same thing for love and hate being the nether sides of each other.

And oh, there were men beautiful as fallen angels, and described as such—not handsome in the conventional sense but truly *beautiful*, often androgynous, some dark as obsidian, others with golden hair that was always my weakness, and tinged with cruelty that was somehow divine. Androgyny and the blending of sexuality and fluidity of gender and the power of demonic desire—oh, how it affected me with its exquisite dark power.

I became in that moment a slave of Tanith Lee, and her entire oeuvre.

And because I was writing at the same time, learning and emerging as a writer, I can honestly say that Tanith Lee was my greatest and most constant inspiration.

Everything I've written has been coloured by the arcane imagery of this amazing mistress of language. Her inner lens filtered the coarse mundane world into a fragile jewel of awe, and it taught me to look for similar solemn beauty in all things.

I admit, for the longest time I tried to copy her—in style, language, and aesthetic substance. I'm certain, in those days, many of us young writers did. But there is only one Tanith Lee, and what my peers and I achieved were merely our own much dimmer variations, until we learned to find our own voices. But of course the inescapable fact is, every apprentice studying at the feet of a master teacher is always influenced by that master's school and carries a permanent stamp of the teacher's spirit.

I am grateful beyond measure that I've been branded by Tanith Lee, and her mark lives inside me, in my language and my visions. In my *Compass Rose* books ('Niola's Last Stand' from *Gods of the Compass Rose*, forthcoming), influenced heavily by the *Flat Earth* books, I speak of a Goddess of Wonder:

'It was said in the desert lands of the Compass Rose that one of the stars was in fact the Goddess of Wonder, for she hid in the velvet abyss of night sky from the relentless pursuit of the Lord of Illusion. And sometimes mortals would find her as their gaze searched the heavens, unwitting... And in that moment they would experience a transcendent pang of joy, a reeling sense of the world's profundity and glory overhead...'

It occurs to me suddenly that this goddess—she is none other than Tanith Lee herself. Thus, even now—even as I write this—new meaningful connections continue to be made!

When I had the privilege of finally making personal contact with Tanith, beginning a correspondence with her in 2007, and ultimately publishing her work via my humble micro-press, it was the culmination of many decades of need and hope. As though a power circuit finally connected, an aspect of my life was made whole— my desire and urge and unresolved search were at last fulfilled.

And when Tanith was taken from us in 2015—only four months after my own mother had died from cancer, in the same year—it was personally devastating, a double loss of family. I recall vividly the conversation on the phone several years ago when Tanith had first told me she considered me one of her Nieces, and to be honest I don't think I quite believed it then—it was just too *vast* and *large* and overwhelming for my mind to take in. But it broke my heart again to be reminded of it when John Kaiine let me know about the plans for this *Night's Nieces* anthology and generously invited me to submit a story. This is such an unbelievable honour. Furthermore, the other wonderful Nieces, in whose bright company I suddenly find myself, are some of the finest writers working today.

And now, about this story...

Tanith's work is so varied, so brilliantly diverse in genre, that many of us probably think of her as 'ours', depending on which of her books we imprinted upon. For many, she is, first and foremost, a Horror Grandmaster and represents the best of horror and dark fantasy. For others, she is the goddess of high fantasy. Others yet, science fiction, historical fiction, gothics, erotica, LGBTQ fiction, lyrical contemporary, etc.

Personally I think I've imprinted on her high fantasy more than anything, followed closely by her history-flavoured horror and science fiction. As a result, the story I've written for this anthology, 'Streets Running Like a River', is coloured in part by *Sung in Shadow*, which is Tanith's retelling of *Romeo and Juliet*, and also by *The Secret Books of Venus*, where alternate Venice is portrayed.

'Streets Running Like a River' is a futuristic story set in

the same world as my *Pantheon* science fiction series (still in planning stages), about a future where all countries are geo-politically isolated from each other and forced to exist behind a kind of 'iron curtain' that I call the Iron Honeycomb. This particular story takes place in 'Venettia, Italia', my own take on Venice, and it has elegant violence, beautiful pride, a world-weary, slightly mad heroine, and many, many swords.

May it convey but a single ember of the bright flame that is the incomparable goddess of the night, Tanith Lee.

Vera—

I LOVED your book. And yes, you are, from what you describe,
a synesthete. We all react differently, but the things you
described in your email are decidedly IT. I didn't know
this was what I was until a few years back. I'd just always
seen numbers and letters in colours, plus certain other
items, like voices, sometimes music sounds, etc: I've only
so far met one other person who had this talent - also a writer. But many famous writers and composers are part of the
club - Flaubert, I think, for one...

LOR was a splendid read. I especially liked and admired
your fast-paced yet imaginatively leisurely creation of the
city - or rather, reporting of it - it seemed quite real.
Also the cameo histories of characters who seemed to arrive
then vanished, but subsequetly played such significant
reprises - particularly Immogen - do I spell that right - forgive me if not, spelling and typing are not my strongest skill,
Your three-sided love-story was also amazing, worthy of a
first class film noire. The ironic, (concocted surely by gods)
first sexual meeting of Ranhé and Elas II was Shakespearian
in its tricks behind schemes behind screens. The bath scene,
steamy in every sense, was quite extraordinary and completely
erotic in the best sense. Their final angry culmination
at the novel's end was sensational. That she subsequently
left him, pawing the ground, was so her, and so possible, and
quite, for me, surprising. I also valued immensely the
belief that comes through the novel of goodness and truth
winning through, a theme often mangled or made clichéed in
fantasy, but here written with great integrity. The world
theme and the love theme match. For Ranhé is deceived by
the power of emotional love, yet comes to know the truth of
earthly physival love, less aesthetic than essential - just
as the rainbow breaks back into the world of black and white.
I have to say your use of the two mediums - black and white
and the emergence of every shade, are both masterly.

Thank you for such a glorious adventure.

Lots love.

Vera Nazarian

I got off the plane at Venettia with two swords. They were poor quality asps, with long thin epee blades that I'd gotten at the airport gift shop in Roma Maiorra before boarding the plane for the connecting flight, having checked in my own unnecessarily—forgetting for a moment it was Venettia I was coming to, the birthland of naked steel.

One of the swords had a tiny uncomfortable three-ring grip, so that I wondered how I'd get my fingers through that contraption, and whoever comes up with these useless designs. Until it occurred to me that the three rings formed a clover pattern, and it was one of the popular House affiliations. Pick one and you automatically become an honorary member for the duration of your stay. And I had now unwittingly affiliated myself with Poventa. The House of the Poor.

I was a thoughtless idiot.

The Houses were advertising again. I had thought that nonsense over and done with, with the coming in power of the Autocratte Rorin. But obviously there were still undercurrents of insurrection.

What a time to be in Venettia!

'Paola!' someone cried, and I turned my head to search

the crowd near the international baggage claims.

A burly man with red-gold hair and beard stood up on his toes like a ballet dancer—as though he needed any help towering over the crowd—and gesticulated to me enthusiastically with his own short dagger, holding it up with insolence by the blade between forefinger and thumb, so that I could see the affiliation. The pommel wore the unmistakable shape of the Moretti rose flower, and with it came a pang of Familial pride, followed by a strange, almost unfamiliar sensation of *warmth* rising. I felt my throat constrict for a second as I thought of my childhood, all coming forth like a bouquet bursting from the fingers of a conjurer, and the colours of earth and antiquity and sweet Italia.

And that man? Could it really be Barto? After all these years, I knew him in a single blink!

Family Italia was around me now, and I was in its bosom again, after nearly a decade abroad, after working on the other end of the Iron Honeycomb—first entrenched in the restricted formality of Gran Britannia for five interminably long years, and then spending close to five more in the gaudy excess of Unified America with its "life on a grand scale"mentality. In both cases, the Houses that employed me were of the highest elite, and yet I felt the inevitable wear on my spirit of having to resign myself to serving not my betters but those who could best pay me.

As far as *what* I was getting best-paid for, suffice it to say that it involved my expert ability to wield deadly steel, and earned me my previously non-existent middle name. I was now Paola "Morte" Moretti, whether I liked it or disdained it. My reputation preceded me in those places, and now that I've returned home, it must needlessly follow me like a plodding mare, or rather a shadow carcass of one.

Now I was to take on brand new employment, unusual in the sense that it was merely a resumption of my original employment while here on my native soil. For, I was still indentured to serve the Chiarenza, and although my obligation to that noblest of Houses was almost at an end, I still had one year of service remaining that I owed to them. Once the year was over, I would be free at last—free to be my own mistress, and free to serve no one but my own House, the ancient and impoverished Moretti.

'Paola! Over here, damn you!'

Again I heard the voice of the bearded red-gold haired giant—indeed none other than Bartolo Chiarenza, who was both an old friend and a very distant cousin of Moretti, here to take me directly to the old city villa of Chiarenza.

By now, warmth was overwhelming. It rose up inside me like the lagoon of Venettia at high tide, filling me to overflowing, at the sight of Cousin Barto.

I raised my hand and waved back at him with the pommel of the Poventa asp, held with equal disdain between forefinger and thumb, while moving through the thick crowd toward him.

'What? What's this crap?' Bartolo exclaimed as soon as I was within reach. 'What kind of pitiful steel defames your proud hand, cousin? Poventa? Your idea of a sick joke?'

'Damn you too, Barto. It's all they had at the gift shop,' I replied—my tired voice cracking, my face transformed with both a shy and somehow giddy smile—meanwhile putting the cheap asp back in its sheath at my waist. Then

I came into his great bone-crunching embrace, while hearing the thump of his dagger slapping my back.

'Ah... What kind of excuse is that? My old Paola wouldn't have touched a Poventa stick with gloves on. What happened to her?'

'Well, blame it on jetlag and exhaustion. Your old Paola is now ten years older and hardly much wiser. Besides, I packed my own steel very carefully away, just as Francisco taught us all those ages ago. How long has it been now? Fifteen years since the old man sleeps on a marble slab in the Moretti crypt?'

Bartolo sighed, and I felt this large frame shudder, as he released me and stood back, examining me—while I took my own time looking him up and down.

'You look good, Paola, *cara*.'

'Ah... and you look much better than me, Barto. I see no gray hairs anywhere, not in your beard, and not on top of that dense orange head.'

Bartolo made a sound that was the snort of a draft horse coupled with the laugh of a drunken jackal. 'Time is my wench, and knows better than to spoil the color of this sexy mane. Now then, how was your flight, *bambina?* And even more importantly, what news of the outside world? What can you tell me?'

I shook my head and headed to the baggage claim carousel, with Bartolo trailing me. 'Now now, you know I can't tell you anything, donkey. Yes, my flight was tolerable and infernally long—thank you for asking—but that's all you get.'

In my reluctance to speak, I was not merely being coy. Since I had just come through that rare terror that was international customs for the second time, after the initial check in Roma Maiorra, and my luggage was originally coming from a foreign plane—even now that I was past that initial hurdle—I was still tainted by the ugly reality of being an *outsider*, and legally required to comply with the Foreign Non-Disclosure Agreement I had signed when I had originally been permitted to leave. Whatever I'd learned on the other side of the Iron Honeycomb, the wall of *information silence* between *here* and *there* had to remain in place, was inviolate, and I had to abide by it, or risk severe repercussions—not only for myself but for those with whom I communicated.

I was thus a pariah, permanently forced to keep my mouth shut about my experiences—all the wonders or ills or idiocies I'd encountered on the outside. And I was going to be considered this kind of special case for quite a long time to come.

A *dangerous* case.

From now on, in so many ways, I was going to be painfully alone.

Indeed, this particular baggage carousel before me—a sadly deserted oasis, sparsely regurgitating items for an elite or unlucky few—was a reminder of my solitary condition. It was serving only my lonely international flight. Almost no one else was coming from abroad like me; most everyone else here in this airport was domestic.

Thinking back, I could've counted the passengers on my flight on one hand, all of us returning from beyond the Iron Honeycomb, all of us tense, sullen, not meeting each other's gazes, ready to be searched, questioned and detained at any moment. And now our few bags were here, sailing in lonely splendor after being processed and thoroughly examined by customs—or better to I say, *sanitized*.

Bartolo simply couldn't appreciate the uniqueness of

my situation. His inability to be careful in my permanently suspect company was stunningly stupid, in addition to being endearing. It struck me again how much I missed this big fool, this gigantic awkward lug of a cousin who had been such a big part of my early childhood.

And yet he went on. 'Ah, come on, *carissima* Paola, don't make me beg! Not even a tiny little nugget of news, of enlightenment?'

'Not even that,' I said, with a thin smile. 'Seriously, Barto, aren't you afraid of the nearest *sacerdote* hearing you ask me this? After all these years that I've been away, nothing's changed. I've no doubt they still lurk in every shadow, and there are probably at least three in this crowd alone, and a fourth riding the damned baggage carousel with the bags.'

'I'll take my chances,' he said, leaning in behind my ear, while I focused my sharp observation skills on the cavalcade of luggage as it circled the conveyer belt.

'Barto,' I mumbled after a few moments of feeling his hot breath washing my neck. 'Give me some space now, okay?'

'Just one nugget...' he whispered persistently. 'Give me one... please. Tell me anything!'

I glanced back at him, then returned my attention to the carousel and said very softly, 'Fine, here's one: the outside world is *crazy*. Absolutely flaming insane. Everyone has gone mad and everyone wants to get out, and no one can. The Iron Honeycomb keeps us all inside our borders until we go stark raving mad with wanderlust.'

Barto exhaled, his breath stirring the hair at the nape of my neck that had fallen out from the loose ponytail.

'What's Gran Britannia like, cousin? Do they drink tea with every meal? Is it true they still have that old senile King?'

'Barto, I'm going to have to plug your mouth with my scarf, if you don't stop,' I mumbled, finally seeing my own two bags emerging from the maw and sailing along the conveyor toward me—a small basic rolling suitcase, and a long, high-end sword case of reinforced military grade materials. Inside it were my treasures—three magnificent swords and four daggers of varying length and designations, all bearing the rose crest of Moretti on their antique pommels.

'Here we go, come to *madre*,' I intoned with satisfaction, leaning forward, and plucked the sword case, followed by the suitcase, from the conveyor.

'So now you have yours, you can toss the Poventa trash, right?' Bartolo nodded to the two cheap asp swords attached to my belt, with their embarrassing clover pommels.

'All in good time.' It was best not to attract undue attention to my own rare quality steel—and hence to *me*— so I chose wisely to keep the asps precisely where they were on my person and ignored Bartolo's taunt.

'Allow me—' And Bartolo took the suitcase from my left hand, knowing better than to try to claim my swords.

'Careful, just don't drop it, donkey, I have some delicate items inside,' I said, as we proceeded to walk from the airport claims area. 'Where are you parked?'

Bartolo snorted again, carrying my suitcase in his large beefy grasp with the ease of a feather pillow, and ignoring the rolling wheels. 'Parked? Is that what they do in airports in Britannia and America? You forgot how it's done!'

'Oh yes, of course...' I shook my head again with another tired but fond smile. 'There's another cousin even now, endlessly circling the airport, right?'

'Naturally.' Bartolo nodded toward the glass outside doors leading to the arrivals and departures drop-off area.

'So who is it? Anyone I know?' I said, as we walked past the security guards and into the bright sunlight of Venettia.

No answer came from my brute of a cousin.

I blinked, carefully maneuvering my sword case around passerby, and allowed Bartolo to take the lead.

The madhouse that was Venettia became apparent already, with a sea of vehicles of all makes and models circling the few lanes near the curb in the usual merry-go-round, horns blaring, *polizia* in uniforms with standard issue multi-sword belts gesticulating with disgust at those who stopped too long at the curb. The noise, the damp air, the ever-present smell of slightly decadent sea-water from the lagoons, the wonder that was Venettia, all clamored together—and this was still only the airport area on the mainland, a few miles from where the lapping waters began...

Ah, I was home.

As I breathed the air with pleasure and nostalgia, a luxury sports convertible pulled up to the curb directly before us. Bartolo waved, and the driver, a truly beautiful young man with long honey-blond hair that shone with gold and copper highlights in the sun, dressed carelessly and fashionably, did not bother to wave back, and merely stared without any enthusiasm. Squinting against the sun glare I saw a very bored face of sculptured lean angles, and nothing but disdain in the narrowed blue eyes—as soon as he very deliberately removed his expensive, polished black sunglasses.

'That's our ride?' I asked, with one raised brow.

'That's your charge,' Bartolo replied with a crafty grin. 'Surprise, *cara!* Come, meet your newest pupil!'

And then he yelled in a bass voice like a trumpet, 'Adonetto Chiarenza! Here you are, and here she is! Come and meet your new fencing master, *Signorina* Paola!'

So—I thought—this was the horrible boy I was to teach for a whole year of my indentured servitude, Adonetto Chiarenza, the spoiled brat eldest son of the Chiarenza, who was going to make my life a living hell for the next many months...

Oh yes, I've heard all about Adonetto, had investigated him thoroughly in fact, while still on my way home, and the conclusion I've come to was a grim one.

The young man was a lazy useless player who spent his days and nights drinking, brawling, and screwing, going from dance club to duel to orgy, and sleeping till four every day, only to repeat the dreary cycle, while his father despaired of him ever becoming suitable to lead his House.

I had my work cut out for me.

The convertible idled at the curb, superbly tuned engine running, and Adonetto did not bother to get out of the car. He merely nodded with insolence, taking in my plain and rather homely travel attire—dark pants pulled over scuffed working boots, and worn jacket over a dowdy grey shirt buttoned all the way up to my throat, where an old scarf looped twice—and waved one hand at me, elegant fingers dangerously close to forming the insulting "thumb" gesture.

'Benvenuto in Italia, signorina. How lovely to have you here, come all this way just for me.' His voice was melodious despite its devastating tone of sarcasm. 'Please forgive me if I don't get up, but you know how it is, airport *polizia* are unforgiving creatures.'

I was certain he also threw a very brief disgusted look at my Poventa asps, but at least, unlike Barto, said nothing.

'No problem, and nice to meet you, Adonetto,' I said with a blank face, after the tiniest pause, giving my new pupil a brief nod. Then I followed Bartolo who went around the back and opened the small trunk. He stuffed my suitcase inside, and then both of us realised there was not enough room for the long sword case.

'I'll take the swords with me in the back seat,' I told Cousin Barto whose sheepish expression in that moment made him look about ten years old, and was ridiculously endearing. Lord, how I missed having Bartolo around!

'So sorry about that, *cara,* I know those precious blades of yours must be kept safe,' he muttered. 'Bah! I didn't think—else we would have taken the big SUV with the bigger luggage area—'

'Relax, Barto, I'll manage.'

I came around and got in the back, with its rather narrow sporty bench seat, trying not to poke or scratch the fine leather upholstery with the scabbards of the two cheap asps still attached ignobly to my person. Then I carefully positioned the sword case containing my real steel on the floor before the empty seat next to me, so that it rested against the back and stuck out slightly, like a strange headless passenger.

Bartolo scratched his ruddy head worriedly. 'Are you

sure you don't want to sit in the front with Adonetto? So you two can get to know each other?'

I shook my head with a tiny smile and motioned for Bartolo to take the front. 'There will be plenty of time to get acquainted later. Besides, you need more legroom. Sit! And let's get out of here before the *polizia* notices us lingering at the curb.'

In reply, Bartolo got in. At once Adonetto Chiarenza revved up the engine with an angry roar. Without a word, his sunglasses were back on, sleek and menacing. In the next breath we jerked into motion, and started moving through the crazy traffic toward Venettia.

A few miles of crawling along a curving verdant thoroughfare on the mainland brought us to the early edges of the city, where land seemed to have lost its mind and gave in to blue sky and water. Here, the lagoon and the canals took over, and the land buses could go no further. Traffic fell off immediately. Meanwhile the remaining convertibles started to switch to the water navigation systems, and transform before our eyes into the *vaporetti* or waterbuses that were the main mode of transport along the canals.

As we entered the water, Adonetto engaged our own vehicle's acqua-nav—retracting the wheels, until the lower shape of the car was now a sleek boat, with the rubber tires recessed on the underside to provide added buoyancy and improve flotation, while a prow sharpened at the nose and a rudder descended in the back near the trunk.

I stared with growing pleasure of familiarity as we slid along the lagoon water surface, almost flying as we cut our path among white frothing churn on both sides of the vehicle. In moments we were halfway across the lagoon, aiming for the heart of Old Venettia.

All the while Adonetto remained mostly silent while Bartolo chattered with enthusiasm and constantly pointed out things and places I knew very well but he was certain I'd forgotten.

The green-brown shadow water surrounded us, in places mysteriously displaying splotches of teal and verdigris, followed by sudden mirror-shards of brightness that was reflected sunlight. I listened to Cousin Barto absentmindedly and watched it lap in wavelets against the peculiar walls of the approaching shoreline formed of narrow walkways around outlying buildings— the endless rows of houses lining up like honor guard, interspersed with occasional breaks leading into lesser canal alleys.

Eventually we approached the wide mouth opening along the exterior shoreline that was the Grand Canal, an S-shaped snake major waterway curling through the city. We entered it swiftly, with Adonetto maneuvering us past a few other *vaporetti* and gondolas at heedless breakneck speed. Frequent bridges swept above us, including the Rialto which I recognized with a bittersweet pang—I had once kissed a man very dear to me, while standing on that very bridge and looking out over the muddy flow of the canal...

We thrust our way onward, cutting the waters of the Grand Canal into a churning foam "open wound" formed by the merciless sword blade that was our vehicle, circling the ancient structures and piazzas toward the Palace of the Doge and beyond it, where the Chiarenza villa reposed in decaying splendor. Then we took a turn into a lesser waterway, and meandered through alleys and past houses opening into secret piazzas and cul-de-sacs. At one point, as the vehicle floated near the sunken steps of a small stone square with a fountain, we were greeted by hoots, whistles, and cries from a minor gang of youths who congregated around the fountain and seemed to know Adonetto from afar and likely recognized his distinctive convertible.

'Chiarenza! *Qua ti voglio!*' one of them cried angrily. 'Hey, over here! Where have you been? I want my money, *stronzo!*'

The same dark-haired young man stood up from his lazy repose on the rim of the fountain and waved with the pommel of his sword, while others stirred around him, and the hoots and whistles increased.

'*Ti amo anch'io,* De Luca!' Adonetto brought one hand to his lips in an air kiss, and yelled back in a ringing insolent voice. 'You know exactly what to do to get it back—it's simple, do what I told you, and I'll pay you immediately. If you don't, then I'll pay you when I see you next... in hell!'

In reply, the dark-haired De Luca spat and hurled back an intricate volley of obscenities. He then ran up to the very edge of the steps before the water began and stood with his sword raised blade up, pointing with it directly at our vehicle which was floating in a slow coasting drift, a mere ten feet away. 'Very well, turn your back and run, coward Chiarenza! Run from me, whoreson, and may you sink deep in the canal and swim with the crap that floats in it! *Figlio di puttana!*'

'Okay, what is going on?' I said in a cautious voice, seeing how Adonetto responded immediately by tightening his lips and revving the motor, and then started to maneuver and park the vehicle at the steps.

'Whoa, whoa!' Bartolo exclaimed meanwhile, staring back and forth between Adonetto and the shore where a small crowd had now gathered as the rest of the youths approached the edge of the sunken steps. 'What are you doing, boy? Why are we stopping? Who are these idiots? Your father hears about this and we are both going to get our asses handed to us—'

'Shut up.' Adonetto cut him off in a hard voice, with only a side glance at Bartolo, and not even deigning to look in my direction. 'I'll take care of this.'

'Adonetto, no,' I said. 'This is not a good idea.'

In response the convertible motor went silent. Adonetto easily climbed out of the driver's seat which was now adjacent to the steps, and jumped onto the shore with an elegant smooth motion born of practice. I observed how he held his primary sword in a loose grip in his right hand while the second remained in the scabbard—not a bad form, but nothing to brag about.

'Adonetto, don't—' My voice sounded far too mild and trailed off, because at this point my clinical curiosity was engaged.

Bartolo and I watched him take a few steps forward with fearless aggression. The gang members immediately cleared a semi-circle around him, and only De Luca remained, facing him directly.

'I am here now. What did you call me again?' Adonetto spoke through his teeth, as he and De Luca began circling each other slowly, both proudly upright, still only posturing.

'Ah, *Madre di Dio...*' Bartolo muttered, sitting up in his seat, and starting to get out of the car.

But I put my hand on his shoulder to stop him. 'Wait.'

Bartolo frowned at me. 'We can't just let this happen,

cara—old Chiarenza will kill me and eat my liver for letting this get out of hand.'

I nodded. 'I know, and we won't. But—just let it play out, just wait.'

Meanwhile the young men—mostly older teens, and possibly young men in their early twenties—made noises of encouragement. 'Fight! Fight!' they chanted, and in seconds various daggers and stilettos appeared, and swords came forth from scabbards—the usual peacock show.

Nine times out of ten, such dick-waving came to nothing, I knew with certainty born of extensive experience. Here in Italia especially, the old anti-sword-violence laws were still being properly enforced.

'I called you a coward, Adonetto Chiarenza,' De Luca said with an inflamed intense expression, and raised his sword in a horizontal position, bringing the pommel up close to his chin in a parody of aiming to shoot, then extended his reach again, taunting the other. 'But you're also a thief. You have what's mine and I want it now.'

Adonetto snorted. 'Matteo De Luca, you are a delusional *pezzo di merda*. I already told you the first time. I'll pay you gladly—all you have to do is get on your knees and kiss my ring in front of Carmelina Sciarretta. If you prefer, it can be underneath the bedroom balcony of Carmelina and she doesn't even have to be present, as long as we have a picture of you doing it.'

Matteo De Luca spat on the ground again. *'Vaffanculo.'*

Adonetto's lips curled derisively. 'Very well. You won't do it, and I won't pay. Have a nice afternoon, *piccione.'*

And then Adonetto insolently turned his back on the dark-haired young man and his comrades and started to

81

walk back to the car. He was followed by hostile boos and whistles of the gang, but ignored them admirably. Just for a moment, I began to think better of him—there was some hope in this boy after all.

In front of me, Bartolo exhaled in relief, and twisted his bulky shape that barely fit in the passenger seat, to lean closer and look at me with admiration. 'You were right, cousin Paola,' he said with a wink, and padded my arm with his large beefy hand. 'The boy can handle himself. And, no harm done...'

His words were cut off when a short, needle-sharp stiletto lodged itself in the side of his throat.

I gasped.

Bartolo froze, gurgled... while blood started pumping rhythmically from his deep wound. With a look of utmost surprise he raised his hand to the wound, reaching for the dagger.

'Barto, no!' I cried, while my own pulse exploded with terrible adrenaline-fueled motion. At the same time, a deep, long-repressed part of me—the part that contained my entire childhood folded up and compressed into a vulnerable ball of *sensation*—was going into ice-cold shock.

'No! Do not touch it! Stop!' I lurched forward in swift reflex, holding up my cousin's gradually slumping body, as he slid back against the seat, choking on blood, his large clumsy hands still trying to hold his own throat. It was my own voice speaking, hard and commanding and professional, but somehow I was floating *outside* my own body, looking down at us in utter disbelief...

'Do not try to pull it out, keep still! Please, Barto—'

In the blink of an eye my gaze scanned the scene, and I saw the smirking youth who threw the dagger—

recognising him from the swift motion his body made, that I'd seen with my peripheral vision, even before it happened. Even now my professional instinct took over.

At the same time, Adonetto, who'd had his back turned to them, now growled with fury, his face contorted, and whirled around, this time raising his sword. He flung himself directly at the one who'd thrown the dagger. A maddened plunge of his sword inside the chest, and the other young man cried out and then collapsed on the steps, while Adonetto pulled his blade out with a fierce cry of satisfaction, and kicked the still-twitching body.

What happened next was a messy brawling horror.

With yells of rage, the youths attacked all at once, and De Luca was the first to reach Adonetto.

I glanced once at my poor beloved old friend Barto, bleeding out in precious seconds, before my eyes. He desperately needed a hospital, *now*—but if I recalled correctly, in Venettia, no ambulance was ever going to be dispatched in a timely manner for one dying man. Besides, there was no time even to make a call.

Right now, this instant, Adonetto, my charge, my pupil, my infernal responsibility, needed help.

Or he was going to be a corpse too.

And so I sprang out of the convertible, landing on the first step above the water, having drawn both the cheap asp blades from their sheaths before my boots hit the ground.

First, I took out the two young men closest to Adonetto, waving their blades uselessly at me. '*Puttana, puttana*, whore!' they called me in initial surprise, even as I pierced both between the ribs on the left side of their chests with a clean economy of motion, so that they were gone before they fell.

While Adonetto's steel clashed rhythmically with De Luca's, I went after the large burly oldest of the youths, who saw me coming and gave me an ugly scowl as he bared two long wide daggers. I disarmed his right hand with a kick, then precisely nicked his left with the blade edge against the inside of his wrist. He dropped the dagger with a harsh cry, in order to contain the sudden gusher bleeding, and I ignored him momentarily to go after two more youths in back of him.

Behind me I could still hear Adonetto, so I could safely ignore him for another few seconds...

Next up—the trio with long dueling rapiers. Their wider, heaver blades would obliterate my flimsy asps, if I'd let them come in direct contact, so no slashes or parries from me—I simply evaded weapon-on-weapon, moving my body out of the way instead, like lightning, and then used the fine points of my sub-par weapons to pierce chests through to the hearts.

Then, things got a little hazy. I was in the zone, moving too fast for my mind to record the sequences, so that there were only targets, lunges, stabs, and opponents falling in their own blood...

About thirty seconds later, there were about two dozen bodies on the ground.

Some of them were even still alive—I needed survivors to make the emergency call and make it worth their while for the ambulance to get here.

But in my mind, *I killed them all*. It was the only way I could stop myself from perpetrating the carnage in reality, imagining them cut up and screaming for what they did to Barto... That, and the fact that I needed them alive for Barto's sake.

Ambulance fodder.

I turned to look back at the car, and Bartolo slumped on the seat, blood pouring out of him and staining the damned leather upholstery. Did the stiletto hit or even nick the carotid artery? A lot of blood, but, hard to tell... A surge of despair washed over me. He wasn't going to make it.

With fury I turned my attention at last to Adonetto and De Luca, both panting and circling each other, thankfully still unhurt. Adonetto must have been aware, with some part of his focused attention, of the carnage happening around him, because he threw me a strange intense look in which I read fear and sudden acknowledgement—and then he returned to his adversary. Once again, their swords clashed and parried...

'Enough!' I roared at them. '*Basta!* Or do you want to die too?'

They paused, and De Luca glared and hurled obscenities at me. But he definitely appeared wary and started to back away.

'No! I'm not done with this piece of crap!' Adonetto exclaimed, brandishing his sword.

'Oh, yes, you are,' I said grimly, reaching out suddenly and grabbing the young man by the ear, and pulling him to me, like one would a five-year-old—realizing with painful emotion that I was doing precisely what old Francesco Moretti would do to me and Barto, all these years ago, separating us during fights by the ear, and causing a small wrenching pain in order to drive a bucket of sense into us.

Adonetto yelped in surprise, completely shocked by what I was doing. He then tried to twist out of my grasp, but I shoved him backward toward the car floating near the steps.

'Get in, idiot, and hold Barto's neck—*carefully*. Use a handkerchief, anything, just do not attempt to pull out the dagger.'

And then I turned to De Luca, stilled in his own version of shock. 'Run!' I told him, since I had plenty of dead and living bodies on the scene already. 'Move! Get the hell out of here, or you will be charged as a perpetrator of all this.'

'Screw you, bitch!'

'Okay, your call.' I shrugged, sheathing one of my swords, in order to reach in my jacket pocket for the small, cheap pre-paid mobile phone—also procured at the Roma Maiorra airport gift shop before departure, and thankfully charged during the flight. I used one hand to punch in the emergency code. At the same time I used my other hand, still holding the second asp, to skewer De Luca through the abdomen, twisting painfully, so that he cried and doubled over, dropping his sword and holding his gut.

The emergency line operator picked up, and I modulated my voice immediately into *helplessness*, raising my pitch an octave higher into a disgusting female cliché, and adding a quivering tone of fear. '—Yes! There's been a horrible incident of mass violence over at—' I looked around for a street sign—'Piazza di Cigno. Please help! At least a dozen seriously wounded and more casualties! Horrible, blood all over! Young men and boys dead and dying! Please, please, hurry! Send ambulances immediately! Blood running into the canal, running in the street, so much blood! *Please!*' I ended on a hysterical weeping note, while the operator tried to console what he thought was a panicking anxious female.

'Yes, help was coming immediately, they were sending out multiple ambulances via airlift helicopter, all was going to be well.'

I hung up the phone, then coldly moved past the fallen dead and wounded, ignoring the moans and cries on the steps near the water. I got into the convertible, where Adonetto was holding Barto's neck with a piece of fabric pressed against his wound.

It didn't look good. Bartolo was passed out, and he was not breathing, and his pulse was almost non-existent, and oh, there was so much damn blood all over the upholstery.

'You—you can help him now, yes? It's going to be okay, right? The ambulance—it's coming—so, is he—is he going to live?' Adonetto started to mutter with a dark expression, all the while looking at me with intensity. All his fear and focus and attention were now in those blue eyes, and all of it trained on me. Not a trace of disdain, and instead a reliance on my authority.

Just like that.

It took death and murder to make the brat begin to respect me, I thought bitterly.

'*Signorina* Paola—'

'Adonetto,' I interrupted him in a hard voice. Then I cast my gaze around the small piazza with its fountain. Noticed De Luca contorting in agony on the steps nearby. Noticed the others, moving, moaning, lying dead. 'See this, Adonetto?' I pointed at the scene.

He frowned, unsure of how to respond, then muttered, 'Yes.'

'This is an act of god.'

Adonetto continued frowning in confusion. 'You

mean—do we tell them it was an accident? It was—'

'What is a god, Adonetto?' I said, watching the tousled golden hair falling around the young, beautiful, stubborn face of the idiot before me.

The young man shook his head, continuing to hold his fingers over Bartolo's throat, with the blood-soaked rag. 'God is the Almighty, and he has judged us here today— is that what we say—'

'Not the Almighty on the ceiling of the *Cappella Sistina*, but *a god*. Listen carefully when I speak to you. Now— what is a god?'

The sound of helicopters came in the distance.

'I am—not sure what you mean, *Signorina* Paola. What—'

I sighed in rising irritation. 'A god, by definition, is one who can experience everything at the same time in a probability set—pain, pleasure, wonder, doubt, anger, love, terror. A god is multi-existential,' I said. 'Are *you* a god, Adonetto? Do you feel all these things right now, as you *exist*? Do you feel hate and love and fear and wonder all at once, for these terribly human boys lying all over the place in various stages of mortality?'

'No...'

Maybe you will someday...

I nodded. 'Then let me tell you—*I* do. I am triumphant and broken and terrified and furious and sad and ecstatic and *deadly*, right now. I am a god, *by my own definition*. And as far as you are concerned, I am *your* god, Adonetto. From this moment on, you do as I say, and you listen to me and you obey. Or I will *destroy* you.'

Adonetto's mouth parted. He was looking at me in absolute fascination. And then he moved his head slowly in the affirmative.

'Good,' I said, letting out a breath. 'Then we are set— for the moment.'

And then I added, as the helicopters became visible overhead at last, and were landing on the piazza around us: 'However, if Bartolo Chiarenza does not survive, I am going to make your worthless life a living hell, for as long as you are my responsibility. Is that clear, Adonetto?'

He blinked in fear and—dare I say—*wonder*. 'Yes...'

But seeing my narrowing eyes, he immediately added, 'Yes, *Signorina* Paola—*dea*.'

Goddess.

But I was ignoring him already, and waving to the EMTs as they filled the piazza, scattering a flock of pigeons that now circled in the distant sky overhead.

Barto was all that mattered in this moment.

It occurred to me, yes, I was definitely home. Home was not merely Italia, but wherever I had to be, by my own definition, fully *divine*.

I had my work cut out for me.

Tanith Lee and John Kaiine

Sarah Singleton

I didn't start reading Tanith Lee's work until I was in my thirties, and already a writer. I began, by chance, with a short story called *The Tree: A Winter's Tale*. I remember the effect it had. Her writing style was lyrical and poetic. Her view of the world was surreal, dark and feverishly beautiful. I wanted more. Next came *Dark Dance*. As soon as I had finished the last page I turned back to the beginning and read it again, then *The Blood of Roses*, *When the Lights Go Out* and *The Secret Books of Paradys*. I had found a writer whose work aligned with aspects of my own interior landscape. Her work was compelling, witty, passionate and erotic. I was soon an avid fan.

I finally met Tanith and her husband John Kaiine at a *Blake's Seven* convention, which I attended with the sole purpose of hearing her talk about her work. I felt some trepidation – imagining that she might be as chilly and aloof as many of her female characters. How wrong I was. From the start, she was warm, funny and kind. We became friends and I spent fascinating times with her. She was a generous host, a brilliant correspondent, supportive in times of personal difficulty, as well as encouraging of my own creativity. She has influenced my writing greatly, but more importantly, Tanith and her work enriched my experience of life.

Le Livre de l'Ambre: City of Gold

Sarah Singleton

August 9

I am travelling to Paradys to meet my lover. The assignation was agreed four, vast weeks ago. How time stretched, each day a century of emptiness. Every night I lay awake haunted by some kind of precognitive ghost, phantasms of the pleasures I dreamt would be mine once these wheels of weeks had made their slow revolutions.

Now the moment is upon me. The journey, by train, is illuminated, the August landscape as brilliant and sumptuous as stained glass. Ripe wheat and gleaming stubble in pale gold fields. Brittle yellow stalks of seeding grass and the architectural columns of dry hemlock and hogweed teeter in the verges. I am tense and apprehensive, my throat dry, my body without any appetite but one. There is no escape now. I am pulled by the unbreakable cord of my longing, through the hours of the journey, to the meeting.

I move through the unavoidable procedures and formalities in the Victorian brick halls of the London terminal, in cavernous gothic tunnels and beneath ecclesiastical archways, all made contemporary with furnishings of plate glass. The train is called and the pressure of the winding cord eases as the journey begins once more, through light, and darkness, and light.

A landscape of huge flat fields, without hedgerows or trees. Villages, towering pylons. Another hour passes. Not long now. The moment approaches, the singularity towards which I am drawn.

And suddenly it is here, the time. He is here. I walk towards him, through a crowd of disembarking passengers who only half exist. He is the locus of the city, from which the rest of it – the grimy, overarching station, the scatter of pigeons, the crowds of travellers and the unfamiliar language – seem to take their being, as though it is a cloak he wears: Paradys – City of Love, City of Light.

I can hardly speak; my mouth is dry. The words rehearsed so long are knotted in my throat. He is beautiful, my lover; strange and familiar. The eons of waiting and longing have worn me away. The image I have conjured so fervently these last weeks now jars with reality. I am not disappointed but feel a shiver of disorientation as the mask of my dreams slides over and then resolves itself into the face of my lover. He takes charge, picking up my bag and leading me to the front of the station. Tall statues with tranquil faces grace the façade. Beneath them, people smoke and talk and wait. We climb into a taxi and drive along boulevards and narrow cobbled streets, under dusty plane trees with faded yellow leaves. Do we talk? I am not sure what we are saying, what slight, meaningless things. I am only aware of the weight of his arm on my shoulders, his face so close to mine, his accent, the faintest scent of his body.

The apartment is in the 19th arrondisement. We pass through a heavy front door and into a tiny elevator to the third floor. The place has dark wooden floors and white walls, two empty marble fireplaces, the affectation of an antique *prie-dieu*, and two chipped altar candlesticks, with chipped gilt paint. The place is comfortably dusty and untidy. My lover opens a bottle of red wine and we drink quickly. He talks a lot, and slowly the wine unloosens the knot in my throat and I talk too. Inconsequential things. The journey, my impressions of the flat, his week at work. Beneath the long windows, open in the heat, traffic slowly passes and voices shout. The air smells of hot tarmac, car exhaust and cigarette smoke.

Sometime later, measured only by the emptiness of the bottle, we determine to leave and wander the city streets. The light in the room changes, as the sun lowers over the grey-lead rooftops. Outside the apartment door, just after he turns the lock and before we step into the elevator, we both pause and look at one another. Almost palpable threads draw us together, but we are motionless. The charge in the air around us builds and intensifies, building towards its inevitable culmination. Then the lift door clangs open and we move again, out of the building and into the streets.

We climb the hill to Montmartre, through narrow streets. Orange geraniums flourish in pots on steps and balconies. Alleys and stairways leap up and fall away in perspectives altered by wine, unfamiliarity and the strain on my nerves.

At the top of the hill stands the Sacred Heart. The huge white church reflects the slanting evening sunlight. The walls and dome seems fragile, like eggshell. Or perhaps like icing sugar, patterned with sugar panes – burnt cherry, dark plum. We stand in front of it, on the white-paved courtyard with its curved balustrade, and Paradys lies before us, into the distance. The iconic iron spike, the coil of the river, the billowing sea of tarnished lead roofs, the punctuation of spires and towers.

Gold in the dying summer light, the beautiful city. Spread with gold. Gilded and burnished. Paradys.

Darkness seems to rise from the river, filling the city with night. Yellow lights in the streets. In the Ile de Paradys we sit in front of the Temple Church, with its vast wheel of a window and eat blisteringly cold chocolate ice cream. It is the first thing I have eaten all day. We drink Cognac in smeared glasses.

My lover's body is slender, the colour of honey. His skin is tight and smooth as a new glove. He falls asleep as we finish, but I lie awake for a long time, exhausted, wired and overwhelmed, drinking up the beauty of him, my lover lying beside me. Outside, in the early hours, I hear the clatter of countless bottles as the recycling lorry trawls past.

When I wake, I am alone. A huge plaster rose, paint-blurred, is attached to the ceiling above the bed. Too apposite to be real, the sound of a piano soaks down from the apartment on the next floor. A woman starts to sing, some aria from an opera I do not know. It is perfect, and unbelievable.

My lover has left me a note on the table in the kitchen, along with a croissant in a paper bag and an untidy handful of banknotes. *Enjoy your day*, I read. *See you this evening. Je t'aime a la folie.*

I spend the day in a daze of lust and exhaustion, light-headed, aroused, walking the city streets. The first thing I do is buy a street map and I chart my progress south, to the river, beginning to claim the lineaments of the city with my feet and memory. By mid-day it is hot but many of the streets are at least partially shadowed. I explore the dim, perfumed interiors of churches, trace the remains of a medieval city wall, and wander in arcades with tiled corridors, chandeliers and gilt mirrors. In the afternoon I secure bread and cheese with my mangled French and sit in the Tuilerie gardens on a green chair, under leaves made dark by the sun. Rooks pace the gravel pathways. As I eat, a young man (dark-haired, Algerian perhaps) approaches with a friendly smile and begins to converse. His eyes are a peculiar tawny-yellow – not unappealing. He invites me for a coffee, which I decline with thanks, and then he asks for my phone number which I decline in the same manner.

'You've visited Paradys before,' he says. When I shake my head, he gives a slight shake of the head and gestures with his hand.

'Yes,' he asserts.

I shrug, not wishing to offend.

When he gets up to leave, with a gracious farewell and a flash of those odd tawny eyes, he returns me the map he has scrutinised with advice for sight-seeing. 'You need a guide,' he says. 'The city is full of angels.'

At first I suspect this is a continuance of his suit, but I'm mistaken. He walks away, and looking on the map I see he has circled a point in the west of the city, close to the river and the old city wall. Is this where he lives? I order a bitter coffee from a stall in the park, and lean back in the seat. I think I sleep for a short time, because the light has changed when I open my eyes. Thin gauzy clouds, tinged with amber, have covered the face of the sky. I pick up the map and start to walk again.

I move into an older quarter of the city. The streets are narrow. The sky is a thin ribbon running between buildings. I see an old cinema with a locked red door, and numerous art and antique shops with dark interiors and the odd tempting gem in the window – a table painted with angels, a knife with a crystal blade. Daunted by the gravity and cost of such goods, I do not step inside. From time to time I stare, open-mouthed and sweaty, into interiors like dark lakes in which, perhaps, inhabitants from another, more refined and ancient world look out to a contemporary surface.

Ahead I see the city wall, a slice of it anyway, wedged between a Brutalist concrete office block and a car showroom selling the kinds of sleek, oversized cars that cruise along the boulevards of the city centre. Have I come so far? I check the street name and discover I have found my way to the place marked by the young man on my map. Of all the places in Paradys, I could hardly have come here by chance.

Beside the car showroom, tucked away, is another antique shop – seeming to specialise in books and prints. Two old men are sitting at a table on the pavement, smoking and drinking coffee beneath a faded yellow canopy. Beside the two men are wooden wine crates full of books and plastic albums full of old postcards. The men stop talking to consider me, then carry on with their conversation. They aren't speaking French. I pick up an album; dozens of postcards of St Jeanne. She is always fervent and beautiful. In some she bears a sword, in others a crucifix, or a banner. Some of the postcards have addresses and messages written on the back, in handwriting from the 19th or early 20th centuries. The second album displays postcards of the southern city, the sea port Marcheval. Grand colonial buildings, north Africans dressed in the livery of servants, a statue of warhorses.

The men have stopped talking again, but they pay me no attention. I brave myself to walk into the shop. It is narrow and crooked, with shelves that seem to overhang. More crates containing sheaves of etchings and prints. Books, dating from the 17th century to the 1970s: old histories and taxonomies alongside ludicrous copies of Playboy; a 19th edition of Machiavelli's *The Prince* next to a paperback of St-Exupery's *The Little Prince*; a first edition of the occult and alchemical *Secret Books of Venus*. These I picked up – impressed by the craft of the 18th century book-binder – the fine-tooled leather covers, the marbled mauve Venusian end-papers, the keen pleasure afforded by the thick, watermarked paper and the printed letters in their antique font – the awareness of the inked metal pressed lovingly to the page. Fine engraved illustrations too: a flamingo impaling a man, the sky marked with a crescent of arcane symbols. I hold the book to my face and breathe the scent of the pages, a perfume with notes of mildew, ink and smoke.

The books are far beyond my means but, surreptitious, I find my phone and take photographs of the books, covers, illustration and printed pages.   As I slip the mobile into my pocket, I see a tatty manila box with a lid, a small metal nameplate on one end, a piece of bristly twine tied around it. I cannot read the tiny scrawl on the browned card in the nameplate but I pick up the box. It is rectangular, about three inches deep, and I feel something slide as the box tilts.

'Take it,' a voice behind me says in French.

I jump, startled and unaccountably guilty. It takes a moment for my brain to unravel the language. 'What?'

'It's for you.'

I'm not sure if I have understood him correctly and we are caught in a stand-off, me half holding out the box, he gesturing for me to keep it.

He tries again, in broken English. 'For you.' He pushes the box toward me.

'How much?' I am fearful of misinterpreting and causing offence, of being accused of theft.

He pushes the box a second time, so it presses against me.

'What is it?'

The man smiles. His teeth are stained. I catch the scent of coffee from his breath. He stands back and ushers me past, through the shop and out into the sunshine.

I

Mathurin, apprentice to the magician Ambroise, ran through the market beneath St Eustache towards his master's house in rue d'Argent. Late in an October afternoon, the market was coming to an end. Blood ran in the gutters from the butchers' stalls. Straw, cabbage leaves and fish guts were trampled indiscriminately into the cobbles. The smell of woodsmoke and tallow blended with the distant reek of ammonia from the tanneries to the east, and the ever-present shit-and-mud breath of the river.

Mathurin, aged seventeen, observed it all. He never spoke much, but he soaked it up, the market and the people. He carried three old books tied with string, and a basket with such magicians' essentials as ink, quills, parchment, fresh cheese, bread, lettuce, garlic and a bottle of red wine. He stopped briefly in the market to buy several plump peaches, then hurried on again. His master's house stood in a narrow alley just beyond the shadow of St Eustache, so their lives were punctuated by the tolling of church bells. The house had only three rooms, and a tiny garret under a tiled roof, in which Mathurin had slept every night for the past ten years. The magician had spotted him drawing pictures in the dust on the street, and impressed by his precocious draughtsmanship, had taken him into his house, his service and his tutelage.

The magician's three rooms were piled one on top of the other, with a narrow wooden staircase to connect them. Mathurin did the cooking in a lean-to in the tiny courtyard at the back. The first floor was the public space – a kind of living and consulting room, with a private study on the second floor and Ambroise's own bedchamber on the third. The exterior was painted a pale, peeling blue, stained with damp and darkened by smoke.

Ambroise was sitting in the consulting room when Mathurin stepped inside. He had a letter in his hand, upon which Mathurin saw the flourish of a signature and a wax seal. Ambroise was reading intently.

'What is it? A commission?'

Ambroise looked up. He was about fifty, still straight and hale with long iron-grey hair and coarse, heavily-lined skin. 'A summons from the son of the Duc de Lesdiguieres,' he said, raising a coal-black eyebrow. The creases around his mouth deepened.

'The Bastard?'

Although Mathurin pronounced it with the name the son was known by on the streets of Paradys, Ambroise gave a disapproving shake of his head. 'The son of the Duc de Lesdiguieres,' he repeated, lifting the letter again.

The Bastard, Jean-Frederic, was not much older than Mathurin but he was well known in the city. The Duc had eight legitimate children, who lived in respectable obscurity in a country chateau with their mother. They would inherit his title and estates. None of these offspring excited the public taste for scandal as the infamous Jean-Frederic. His illegitimacy made him more tantalising still. *Of course he is wicked. What would one expect from the fruit of fornication?* The only son of a wild Italian *marchesa* – a beautiful, impulsive girl who had ignited the passions of the Duc and became his mistress for a year before causing a scene when she was unceremoniously cast off – Jean-Frederic enjoyed a life of wealth without duty, and power without responsibility. All this Mathurin knew from talk in the markets, shops, inns and street-corners of the city.

'When do we go?'

'Tomorrow night.' Ambroise did not seem excited by the prospect. 'Brush down my cloak and clean my boots,' he said. 'Collect a clean shirt from the laundry, and make yourself respectable.'

Just after sunset, a boatman rowed them along the river to the Ile de Paradys and the great Temple Church, under a faint half-moon. On foot, they crossed the bridge and made their way through wider, cleaner streets towards the residence of Jean-Frederic. He lived with his mother within a stone's throw of the Palais des Tuileries. Ambroise and Mathurin arrived at a building fronted with marble in the Italianate style. A servant took them along a white-tiled corridor through the house, and out into a cloistered courtyard, where candles already burned and wine waited in a carafe. Ambroise had sipped abstemiously through half a glass when a disturbance and flurry within the house alerted them to the arrival of the host.

Ambroise rose to his feet. They all bowed. The young nobleman wore a lilac doublet embroidered with tiny flowers and pearl buttons, with starched lace at the collar and cuffs, a gold band on his finger, another in his ear. Jean-Frederic was soon deep in conversation with the magician, while Mathurin stared at the celebrated libertine.

Jean-Frederic was beautiful. Perhaps he favoured the *marchesa* because his hair was inky black, longer than was generally fashionable and his face, while pale, possessed a classical proportion, like the plaster copies of Roman statues Mathurin had seen in a studio. His skin was clean-shaven, his lips full and of a pink so deep Ambroise suspected they were painted. The young man's voice was low and smooth, his intonation musical. His eyes were strange though – a pale brown, like almonds. When the young man leaned forward, Mathurin caught the scent of orange blossom and earthy ambergris. How was it possible, he wondered, for this clear-skinned angel of a man to have committed the depravities attributed to him on the streets? The dissolute feasts, the parade of mistresses, the succession of duels in the Bois de Boulogne, the careless gambling and epic fornications?

The sky shaded from deep blue to black, and the moon brightened, rising over the courtyard. The three men dined on rare beef, spiced onions and white bread. They drank more wine. Mathurin sensed that Ambroise and Jean-Frederic were testing one another, at first polite and cautious, then incisive and probing. Jean-Frederic was well educated, but his knowledge exceeded that of most young noblemen. He spoke Russian as well as Latin and Greek, was well versed in Chinese art and poetry, had travelled not only around Europe but also through North Africa and into Persia. Ambroise was evidently impressed. His early reserve melted into passionate discourse. The older and young man argued about alchemy. Jean-Frederic pressed Ambroise to tell him what he knew about the magician from Albion, John Dee, who served at the court of the Virgin Queen.

The hours passed. The moon disappeared. At midnight, Jean-Frederic dismissed the servants and became serious.

'You wish to know the commission I have for you,' the young man said.

Ambroise waited.

'You are the finest magician in Paradys – some say, in all of Europe. I have followed your work for over a year.'

Ambroise gave a barely perceptible nod. 'What do you want?'

'In your writings you speculate that what we observe as reality may only be one such – that we inhabit one sphere which may interlock with, contain or be contained by many other spheres, each its own complete universe. You have proposed that occult events may simply be those points at which these barriers are weak, or even deliberately broken. The peasants' superstitions – fairies, ghosts and the like – may be glimpses into these other spheres.'

Ambroise was sitting very still. His face gave away nothing. His views were unorthodox and possibly heretical, however carefully he couched them to comply with the dictates of the Mother Church.

Jean-Frederic leaned forward, his elbow on the table, his face only inches away.

'I want you to capture one of these creatures,' he said. 'I want you to break through and bring it back, contain it, give it to me. A being from another sphere – whatever it is. I want you to find a way.'

Ambroise still didn't move but his gaze seemed to intensify. 'I don't know if it is possible,' he said.

'But you don't know that it is impossible.'

Ambroise inclined his head.

'You have given glimpses beyond this sphere,' Jean-Frederic said. 'To the Duc of Orleans, and to Normandy.'

Mathurin observed the pulse throbbing in his master's left temple. He looked tired, the lines on his face deeper, his strong hands showing signs that soon they would be the hands of an old man.

'You will never have to worry about money again,' Jean-Frederic said. 'You will remain under my protection and patronage for the rest of your life. You can pursue your own investigations without having to perform tricks for fools. You can write without fear of persecution.'

Ambroise took a deep breath. 'Let me consider,' he said. 'I will send my apprentice with a letter tomorrow.'

Jean-Frederic smiled and stood up. He and the magician bowed, and then the young man was walking away, back into the house, where a woman (his mother?) was waiting. Ambroise stared after him, into the dark.

'He is not what I expected,' Ambroise said.

Mathurin waited for elaboration but none was forthcoming.

August 10

My lover is late.

I am waiting alone in the apartment, sitting on the curved couch, staring at the dusty *prie-dieu*. I sent a text half an hour ago. I cannot read; my focus is lost. My heart and body feel the pain of his absence. This hurt is physical, deep in the gut. Lovesick. What stew of biology – adrenalin, dopamine and the rest – has felled me? The absurdity and the intensity of the feeling both pains and intrigues. One part of my mind, still cool, observes the rest and makes sardonic remarks. *Well, look at you.* To be in love. It is utterly banal. I am humbled.

The manuscript lies on a low table but I cannot read anymore.

I opened the box when I returned to the apartment. A procession of scents, like ghosts, streamed out when I lifted the lid. Old paper, horse dung, coal dust, perfume, brandy, and that aftershave, what was it called? Old Spice. An archive laid down over decades, so many particles of scent clinging to the pages I could now see within the box. A more acute archaeologist of the olfactory could have calculated the decades, or centuries, when the contents of the box were created, read or added to.

I lifted out the piles of paper, some loose, some bound, and they slid over each other, seemingly alive and trying to escape. One heavy clump fell with a thud. Another pile fountained away from my hand in individual sheets and splashed over the floor. I sorted through them. How perfect. How *enchanting*.

Postcards – some written on and some blank, ranging from the 1890s to the 1970s (the Old Spice?). A spiral-bound notebook containing page after page of shorthand notes I was unable to read. Photographs of various tourist locations in Paradys. Sheets of newspaper from the 19th century, a handful of letters in their envelopes, a copy of *Vogue*. The bound pages I picked up last. A typescript. Literally this – not a print-out but the fruit of a manual typewriter (occasional ink smudges, some letters more firmly and boldly keyed than others, mistakes scored through with x's). Written in English, a title – 'The City of Gold' – and a story I began to read at once. A Renaissance city, a magician and a wicked nobleman, a challenge set.

My mobile flares. A message has arrived. *Home soon. Seven thirty. Je t'aime.* I have been staring into space, caught in the fading light of the room, in the amber of longing. I tidy the papers into the box and tuck it beneath the table. My lover will be home in twenty five minutes. For the first time I notice the tick of the flaking gold clock on the mantelpiece (some flea market find, to go with the candlesticks). I am waiting for him to be here, yearning for the tunnel of twenty five minutes to be over. The clock ticks, marking off the measured moments of my life, and I am wishing them gone. Slower the time moves, and slower again. I am burning away time. I think about this equation of love and time but it is another banality. When is anything authentic or new? But it is new to me.

He arrives, my lover, at seven forty. I am almost beside myself by then, worn to a ravelling, burnt away. When he steps through the door, looking tired, I embrace him and rabbit on about my day, make him coffee, suggest preparing a meal. I struggle to manage the intensity of my feelings. I know he doesn't feel the same way and that I am unhinged. I wish he felt the same way. *I wish.* What is it that I want from him? Something I want more than anything, something so vital it has turned over my thoughts, my endocrine system, the chemistry of my brain. Something essentially biological which, at the same time, has opened locked gates to undiscovered kingdoms I sense within and around me. I cannot articulate these feelings. My lover looks helpless when I try to explain. He doesn't know what I am talking about.

He revives after coffee and says we will be eating out. In bed that night, time expands and holds us, without moving. The clock stops. An eternal hour. The night of gold darkens, to black and then to a filthy, flaming red. I don't remember falling asleep.

The next day I wake alone. Half the day has gone. I put the typescript into my bag and head out into Paradys. I find the old cemetery to the north of the city and spend an hour wandering the buckled steps and grave pathways between upright mausoleums with tiny stained-glass windows. In the heat, the trees seem withered, leaves a premature lemon yellow, dropping to the floor. Mournful statues lean in bindings of ivy. I sit on a warm paving stone, lean my back against a headstone and take out the manuscript.

II

A man in the rain.

Mathurin observed him through the window of the magician's house. It was January, and the weather was bitter. Slush lay on the ground from the snowfall the previous week. Filthy with soot and dirt, slush seeped through boots and bit feet.

Since accepting the commission, Ambroise had stopped all other work and spent his time in research and travel. Various strange deliveries arrived, billed to their patron: books, stones and (most often), mirrors and pieces of glass. The costs spiralled. Some days the magician was fired up. On others, he seemed to have aged ten years as though the old man he would be had stepped back in time to swallow him up.

The man in the rain. Water dripped from his hair and had soaked through his cloak. Mathurin took a tense breath. Should he invite him in? Why didn't he knock on the door if he'd come to visit Ambroise?

In the afternoon, rain gave way to flurries of snowflakes. Mathurin built up the fire in the middle room. When he went back to the window to close the shutters he saw the man had gone, and that Ambroise had arrived.

Mathurin told him what had happened as they dined on salt pork.

Ambroise continued to eat but his face acquired a certain stiffness. 'The Church,' he said. 'They've caught wind of something.'

'But the Duke's son said...'

'That we would have his protection? Yes. That doesn't mean the Church is oblivious. And even a Duke is not beyond the power of the Church.'

'Are you worried?'

Ambroise shrugged. 'Yes and no. Our observer clearly wanted to be seen. That is the message.'

Over the following weeks, Mathurin sometimes sensed he was followed. Other men would stand outside the house. Although no-one spoke to him, nor to Ambroise, a sense of threat hung over them. The deliveries slowed. Ambroise spent long hours in his room reading, pacing, talking to himself. Mathurin was given little insight into the process. Ambroise dismissed his questions and kept his work to himself.

Spring embroidered its way through the city: blossom on cherry trees, violets in the cemeteries and parks, moist leaves on the trees beside the river. Spring lambs arrived from the countryside to the markets and slaughterhouses of Les Halles for Easter. As the temperature rose, so too did the stench of the tanneries along the river and the dye factories beyond them.

The nights drew short. In June, Ambroise took complex instructions to the house of Jean-Frederic and spent an entire night explaining his plans. Mathurin accompanied his master but waited in the servants' rooms during this long meeting. He fell asleep on a bench and was woken just after dawn by a girl reviving the fire in the kitchen. He was eating cold meat and bread with the other servants when Ambroise, grey-faced and hollow-eyed, came to fetch him.

'Why don't you involve me?' Mathurin asked, as a boatman rowed them along the river.

'It's uncertain and dangerous,' Ambroise answered. 'In so many ways.'

'Then why are you doing it?'

'Because no-one has ever done it. And because I am old. Old men should take risks.' Ambroise looked away. Mathurin sensed fear winding its way through him. On the far bank, a glossy crow picked at something soft and dead.

In the days before midsummer, wagons arrived at the house in rue d'Argent. Mathurin was given strict instructions on packing up the mirrors and pieces of glass. He wound them in pieces of linen and placed them in wooden crates padded with straw.

Mathurin could barely sleep, those last few nights. He sweated in the garret underneath the tiled roof, disturbed by the heat but also by lurid dreams and a palpable sense of fear. The atmosphere in the magician's house built day by day. Mathurin tried to analyse it, this creeping, itching, growing sense that seemed to condense on the air. He had never encountered it before, in its purest sense, but he recognised it. His flesh and bones reacted against it. His polluted thoughts tended to filth and pain. One night he woke up from a nightmare of torture and dismemberment, of liquid plague pits, of ordure and graves coughing up the corrupt dead. And when he woke, horrified to discover he was aroused and abusing himself, he got up, ran into the street and vomited in the gutter.

Yes he knew what it was. Before sleeping, Mathurin got on his knees and prayed, repeating the *Pater Noster* over and over again, crossing himself. Should he leave the house and run away? Day by day he asked himself the question – but he was held by loyalty to his master, and a compulsion to stay the course.

On Midsummer's Eve Ambroise took Mathurin on a walk along the river. They stopped at one of the taverns.

'It will be tonight,' Mathurin said.

'Yes. But you do not need to come.' The magician's wrists were thin inside his cuffs. The skin of his face sagged, the iron-grey hair becoming white. 'I cannot be sure what will happen. You know the energies I have engaged. It may be fatal for us. It may be worse than that. Jean-Frederic and the rest? They can take their chances. But you, Mathurin.' The older man looked at the younger intently. An almost imperceptible softening of that hard face: 'You're a son to me. As beloved as any son could be. You have a pure heart. You have a future. You don't have to be a part of this. I would prefer you were not.'

Mathurin's hands, hidden beneath the rough table, gripped one another. 'I will come,' he said. 'I won't leave you now.'

A grand house in the woods beyond the city wall of Paradys. Carriages arrived in the early hours of the evening. Other guests arrived on horseback. They were all men, all wealthy, in silk doublets and hose, starched collars, embroidered cloaks. Slashed sleeves revealed glimpses of scarlet and indigo linings. Leaves and petals were stitched onto collars and cuffs.

The guests dined outside at a long table beneath a huge oak tree. A nightingale began to sing, long, plangent notes, as the first dishes were brought out. Soups, then roast meats, lamb and pork, pigeon and chicken. In the middle, facing one another, a roasted peacock with its tail plumage stuck into the cooked flesh, and a swan, similarly decked out with its own feathers. The men drank copiously. Within this quiet environment their voices sounded loud.

Mathurin observed them, standing at a respectful distance with the other servants. The men were all ages – several young, like Mathurin and Jean-Frederic, but every decade was represented, even an elderly man who must have been in his seventies. Listening attentively, he found out this man was the Duc himself, Jean-Frederic's estranged father; the man who had abandoned his mother. Why was he in attendance? Was this escapade designed to tempt the Duc into a reunion with his son?

The talk was frivolous at first, then ribald, and finally serious. The cooked meats were taken away, to be replaced by sugared fruit and marzipan sweets, then cheese, and always more wine to drink. The sun sank by degrees, behind the trees and through a thin veil of cloud so the light changed moment by moment. A horned moon, butter coloured, rested on the tree-tops. The slanted light painted the garden green and gold.

Jean-Frederic, who had been sitting at the head of the table, now stood up. He nodded to the others, pushed his chair back and led them away. The men, about twenty of them, walked beneath the oak tree along a narrow path to the back of the house. The trees thickened then opened into a clearing. The men were silent. A structure of wood, a little taller than a man, stood in the middle with cloths draped over it. Mathurin heard the rippled song of the nightingale begin again.

The evening had slipped into an eerie, midsummer gloaming. The cusp of day and night. The hinge of the year.

Ambroise, dressed simply in black, touched Mathurin's arm. Together they walked into the centre of the clearing and drew back the linen cloth.

Someone whispered but was quickly quiet again.

Mathurin felt, like a breath, the sinister influence leaking from the structure. Ambroise blinked at Mathurin. 'It isn't too late,' he whispered. 'You can still leave. There would be no dishonour in it. You have come this far.'

Mathurin's mouth was dry. He crossed himself and shook his head. 'I'll stay.'

The guests walked around it. What could they see? A labyrinth of mirror and glass. A web of light and reflection, magnification and distortion. From certain points it was invisible, reflecting the surrounding trees so perfectly the structure itself seemed to vanish. From other points, it was black – a void. Elsewhere it seemed to offer impossible views of the house, a magnified moon, the guests themselves, though distorted. The guests were unnerved. Some resorted to posturing and jokes. Others were quiet and cautious. Mathurin suspected that they too were sensing the atmosphere leaking from the heart of Ambroise's creation. Jean-Frederic was standing alone, away from the others. He had a peculiar light in his eyes. Excitement? Victory?

Mathurin instructed the men to stand in a circle around the glass and mirror structure. He sensed the men hadn't noticed him till this point in the evening but they glanced at him now. Jean-Frederic joined the circle last, standing at the place where the mirrors revealed the void. Ambroise nodded to Jean-Frederic, and then to Mathurin. He stepped into the mirrors and disappeared.

The men on the same side looked at one another.

'A trick of the light,' one said. They were nervous. 'What happens now?'

Something shifted inside the structure. The mirrors glittered. Mathurin was not standing as close as the others, but he felt a thump in the chest. Something pushed out at them, a fist of air. Almost instantly, the force reversed and pulled them forwards. A man gave a high-pitched scream. Beneath the surface of a glass, Mathurin saw a face grimacing, something monstrous, white as dough, pink-eyed, with a long, toothless mouth that yawned open. It pressed against the reverse side of the glass and another man screamed, backing away, covering his eyes. Now all the mirrors were moving: monstrous faces, vistas of hell, creatures crawling one over another to reach the surface of the mirror. Then the mirrors went dark.

Mathurin's entire body was shaking. He felt heat on his face, and blood from his nose. His skull ached. Only the clearing existed, and the structure at its centre. Beyond the circle, all was grey and indistinct.

The air heated. A moment later, frost formed over the glass surfaces. The stitched flowers on a man's jacket slithered around his sleeve. Beneath the earth, Mathurin sensed the movement of giant beasts. He glanced at the others. What did they see? Only Jean-Frederic seemed unperturbed, the glimmer of triumph in his eyes. And Ambroise. Where was he?

Everything was still – a moment of retreat, the water's drawing back before the crash of the final catastrophic wave. A fork of lightning leapt up from the ground, like a lance. A mirror cracked, and another. Then, as one, they all exploded. Thousands of tiny, glittering fragments flew out. The men shouted, turning away, covering their faces as glass scored their skin.

Slowly Mathurin turned back and lowered his fingers from his eyes. The structure was gone. Ambroise remained standing, and beside him, on the ground. The creature.

August 11

The city has altered. Walking the streets of Paradys, I see the faces of different cities. Paradys is ancient. Paradise, Paradis. City of Light. City of Love. Beneath my feet lie the bones of Roman slaves, the dried up privies of medieval weavers, oyster shells from their dinners. Along the river I wonder about the old dye factories and tanneries. I see the ghosts of two Nazi officers in a café where two streets meet. I wonder about the magician's apprentice, the quiet observer of a heresy, an unspeakable desecration. The story has infected me. The ink-printed words inhabit my mind, colouring my view. The story opened views on other worlds. It won't let me go. The story is shaping me; telling me.

I hold three postcards in my hands, from the collection in the box. The first shows an artefact from a small museum, which I have located in the centre of the city. It stands in a narrow lane, between tall buildings with closed shutters. A glossy banner over the door announces an exhibition of religious art.

I am one of only a handful of visitors. The museum houses an eclectic collection of art and religious paraphernalia. I pass faded wooden statues of the Virgin Mary and blackened oil paintings of the crucifixion. I show my postcard to an elderly man with a museum lanyard and he directs me to another room. In the centre, under glass on a display stand, is a huge golden monstrance. It stands like a miniature sunburst – a fluted column suspending the circular display for the Eucharist, and the beaten gold flames all around it. Large drops of quartz and amber are embedded in the stand and bubble over the column. It is absurd, gaudy and gorgeous. I hold up the postcard and compare. Although the picture is black and white, this is evidently the right one.

'It was given to us following the closure of the monastery.' I hear the soft voice of the elderly museum assistant. He is standing beside me.

'The monastery of St Michel,' I read from the back of the postcard. No hand-writing on this one.

'It served as a facility for the insane,' the old man says. He is small and neatly formed, his English flawless, barely accented. 'The monks cared for them with more kindness and compassion than many such institutions in the 18th and 19th centuries.'

I am looking for a connection with the story of the City of Gold.

'May I take a picture?' I take out my mobile.

'You already have one.' He gestures to the postcard. Does he think I want some kind of grotesque selfie-with-monstrance?

'I want the colour,' I say. 'The colour.'

III

The creature.

Nobody spoke, or even seemed to breathe. Around them all, an unearthly hush.

The creature lay curled on the floor, sodden-looking, as though it had drowned. Attached around it were huge filmy cloths, layered one over the other, translucent and veined. These lay collapsed and wrinkled on the earth, like fine sheets of silk soaked in dirty water. Mathurin imagined the fairy had come from an ethereal realm of purified air. Here, in the corrupt, phlegmatic atmosphere of earth, its wings collapsed, useless and broken.

Beneath the drenched silk, the creature's body was a drained white. It appeared to be naked, apart from the covering of wings. Taller than a man, very slender and finely formed with long slightly reptilian fingers. Its gender was hard to tell. Perhaps it had none.

Finally Jean-Frederic broke the silence. 'What is it?' he said. 'Is it alive? Stand it up.'

His words broke the spell. The other guests, still bleeding from the shower of glass, babbled to each other.

Mathurin hurried to his master, careful not to tread on the spread of wings.

'Help me,' Ambroise said. The creature was awkward to pick up. Its long body was slippery. In one agonising moment Mathurin stood on the wings and felt a tearing. A burst of fine, golden liquid fell on his boots but instantly evaporated. The creature's body quivered.

'Be careful!' Ambroise said.

Mathurin hated himself.

Finally the creature was held upright. Its head drooped on the stem of its neck. The face, like glazed porcelain, had a tiny nose and mouth and two large-lidded, closed eyes. Long, soaked, treacle-coloured hair fell from its head to its waist. Perhaps in its own sphere, this hair was light too, like the wings.

The old Duc stepped forward. He raised his hand to touch the fairy's face while the other men watched. Though the creature was light, the effort of holding its peculiarly proportioned and unnatural body was considerable. Beyond this, he knew they were all doing something unspeakably bad. What corrupt power had Ambroise tapped to drag this perfect being into their world? And he, Mathurin, was complicit. It was curse on him. For the rest of his life he must bear it, his part in this.

The creature shifted slightly. The Duc pushed its hair to one side to reveal a smooth, lightly muscled chest. He pressed his palm against the shallow breast, and then, emboldened, ran his fingers between its legs. A murmur broke out amongst the watching men. Mathurin realised, to his shame and horror, that he was aroused. The Duc turned round and shrugged at the other men.

'I have no idea what gender it is, this beauty, or if it has a gender at all. But we can still fuck it.'

The murmur rose into a roar.

Mathurin turned to his master in a panic. 'What are they saying?'

Two of the guests pulled the creature away from them, tearing the wings again. Another drew out his dagger and held it to Mathurin's throat.

'Step back old man.' He addressed Ambroise. 'Your work is done.'

Mathurin shouted shrilly so the guest sliced the skin of his neck with the blade. 'Do that again and I'll open your throat,' he said.

The creature was pushed down, face to the earth. The men pulled open their clothes. The old Duc went first. When he tore into the unearthly body, the creature opened its eyes and screamed. The sound was unlike anything Mathurin had ever heard – pure, piercing, resonant – expressing a violation profound enough to crack the foundations of the Earth.

August 11

The second postcard takes me to an old church beyond the walls of the city, in the vast suburbs. This postcard was sent to an address in England. The message is brief, written in English: 'Splendid church window.'

The main doors are locked but a side door is open. Inside an old woman is sweeping the tiled floor. She addresses me in French with a nod and a smile, then continues with her work. The church is dilapidated with damp stains and peeling paint but fresh yellow roses stand in a huge vase before the altar. And there it is – the splendid window.

The archangel, St Michel. He is dressed in golden armour, with swan-white wings behind him and a fiery sword in his hands. The style is art nouveau, the face plaintive, the lips plump and bow-shaped. Behind him, filling the round window, is a circle of flame.

I sit on a long wooden bench. It is only a story, but the angel crystallised in glass stares through me.

IV

Torches and the sound of horses' hooves. Jean-Frederic, who had not yet violated the creature, backed away.

'Who is it? What's happening?' The other guests fumbled for their weapons.

The creature lay, broken and silent, on the trampled ground.

Around thirty men appeared on horseback, all dressed in black. The guest with his blade to Mathurin's throat pushed him away and ran to join the others, swords drawn, in the centre of the ring of horses.

'Throw your weapons down.' The men were calm and strong. The horses stood like statues. Moonlight glinted on their silver bits and stirrups.

'Throw down your weapons,' the voice said again.

Mathurin could not be sure which of the men had spoken. The guests were wild and breathless after their debauch. In the torchlight, they appeared like gaudy dolls. One of the guests flailed wildly with his sword but he was cut down efficiently, with a single thrust.

The Duc stepped forward. 'Do you know who I am?' he said. 'You have not the authority for this.'

'Take him,' came the commanding voice. Two of the horsemen dismounted and took hold of the Duc. One Mathurin recognised as the man who had stood outside his master's house in the winter months.

The Duc protested again, calling on the name of the King, but his captor belted him across the face with his fist. Jean-Frederic had melted away, seemingly invisible to the men of the Church.

Another of the men dismounted and placed his cloak over the creature. He and another of the churchmen talked quietly between themselves.

Ambroise pressed his fingers into Mathurin's shoulder. 'Go now,' he hissed. 'You have a chance. Run before they see you.'

'You run too. We can escape them together.'

'It is too late for me,' Ambroise whispered. 'If they get you, you will face the Inquisition. Torture and death. Go now. Go!' He pushed Mathurin away, towards the trees and the dark. Mathurin turned back to see Ambroise confronted by one of the horsemen. Ambroise drew out his dagger. Mathurin expected him to hand it over but instead – with one quick, strong, deadly move, he cut his own throat. In the torchlight Mathurin saw a rush of darkness from the wound.

His master remained upright for a moment before collapsing onto the ground.

August 11

The third postcard takes me to a house with a walled garden in the old city. The hand-written message (different hand-writing) says only *house in rue de S Agnes*. The wall is too tall to see over. I glimpse the tops of trees. A narrow iron gate on the west side yields a view of overgrown shrubs, rambling roses and the trunks of three coarse trees. In the centre of the garden is a rusty garden table with two once-white chairs. I wait for several minutes at the gate, wanting to make a connection but not seeing it. My feet ache. I need to go home.

At the Metro station I see a beggar with bare feet and long grey hair. His hands are filthy. He asks for money, and I oblige. Later, as though intelligence has passed through the network of the itinerant, a Romani woman with a small child asks me for money, and two minutes after, a teenage boy, punky and perhaps high on something, the cords of his neck visible beneath the thin, bluish skin of his throat. I stare into the face of each of them, looking for something. If the creature remains in Paradys, surely it will be one of these.

When I emerge from the Metro, graffiti on a concrete wall reads '*C'est l'enfer.*' Hell on earth. A poster for a concert in a church shows a stained glass angel dressed in blue.

My lover is already home. He is waiting for me this time. We kiss and embrace. I hadn't realised how late it was.

We prepare pasta and creamy garlic in the tiny kitchen. My lover is tired, his face all shadows. After we have eaten he asks me what I have been doing.

I tell him about the box and summarise the story. He is intrigued.

'The story isn't finished,' I say. 'The writing ends there, but it isn't over.'

'What do you think happens next?'

I describe the clues provided by the postcards and the places. I discuss the dangling threads. The creature was taken by the church. Did they lock it away? Might it have become some kind of angel or saint? Was it confined in a monastery or secret church establishment? Jean-Frederic – what was his role? He fades at the end of the story. Although he commissioned the summoning of the creature he didn't take part in its violation. Is it possible he set up the entire scheme to trap the others? Was he taking some terrible revenge on his father? Was it he who summoned the church officials? Was it even possible that Jean-Frederic, described in all his seductive beauty from the point of view of young Mathurin was not a man at all, but a woman, taking revenge on the men of his (her) class for the discarding of a mother, for her own dubious position as an illegitimate girl child, or for some sexual mistreatment meted out to her personally? What happened to Mathurin? These are all wild speculations.

'I have a feeling,' I say, 'that the creature is still here somewhere. Trapped in Paradys.'

I think of the angel in the stained glass window, the locked garden of the house, the monstrance in the museum – the trail pursued by the person or people who had collected the information in the box I had found. Was I led to this box by the man with the tawny eyes? If so, why me? How did the monastery for the treatment of the insane connect? Did the creature survive its "protection" by the church, only then to be held among the mad? Where was it now? Was it connected to the beggars I had seen in the streets, or the graffiti on the Metro wall?

My lover listens to me talk, on and on. He doesn't interrupt. Finally, when I stop, he asks to see the box and the manuscript.

When I put it on the table in front of him he sighs and takes the papers out, one by one. He turns over the postcard and reads the notes and information. He glances at the letters, the magazines and newspaper pieces.

'It doesn't mean anything,' he says.

'What about the story?'

'You have a story that someone wrote and didn't finish. But the way you talk – you think it's all real? It is just a story. A nasty story. Who would write something like that?'

The structure of thoughts and dreams I have created over the last two days starts to fall apart.

'It all links together.'

'No it doesn't. This stuff – it's all rubbish. Maybe someone emptied out a drawer at work and stuffed all the bits in a box.'

I have spent the afternoon looking for the creature, a being I imagined haunting the city still, trapped here, unable to escape or die. I have tried to see through the surface of things to the truth underneath. I tried to see through the quotidian city to the dreams and stories that hold it together.

'Why don't you understand? Why can't you see?'

'See what?'

'There is more to it.'

'More of what to what?' He sounds angry, sensing I need something from him that he doesn't know how to give. 'I'm tired,' he says. 'I've been working all day.'

'Please don't do this.'

'Do what?'

'Destroy my story.'

My lover stares at me. 'I don't understand what you want.'

And truth be told, I don't know what I want either. Or at least, for a moment I am unable to articulate it. For this isn't simply about the story, or the box, or a creature that might or might not still live in the forgotten corners of Paradys. It is about something else. It is connected to the love I feel for him, which is so vast and precarious it feels as though I balance a giant glass bubble in my hands and every moment I fear this bubble might shatter, and balancing it takes all my thought and energy. And if it falls, if I drop it, I would be the one to shatter. A kingdom would be destroyed. But what is it based on, this love that took hold of me so suddenly? Isn't that just an invention, a story? The truth is I want him to share the story. If two people believe it, then doesn't it become real?

'Come on,' he says. 'Let's go outside. Just for a walk.' My lover holds out his hand.

'But you're tired.'

'Just for ten minutes.' He sighs. 'I want you to be happy.'

I stand up, and we walk out of the apartment. As we wait for the elevator, I remember that moment only days before when we were held in a second of tension, wanting to touch the other. It is there forever, a ghost on the landing, that focused moment.

Outside, the sun throws golden shadows all around us. We walk along the pavement to the dry little park at the end of the road. At the top of the hill is a rocky peak with a wooden balcony. The elevation offers views of a shabby artificial pond and then beyond the park, a vista of the city. Pewter-coloured roofs, countless chimney pots, the sea of receding forms, and in the distance, just discernible, the inverted Y of the iron tower, icon of the city.

September 21, Paradys

My Beloved,

Last week I spent some time reading through the papers in your box. Most of them seemed like irrelevant rubbish, but I asked a friend to interpret the shorthand notebooks. They were written about fifteen years ago, and relate to the story. The research notes concern the young apprentice, Mathurin. The writer of the notes claims to have found papers in a hospital for the insane based in an old monastery. I have rewritten them for you, to the best of my ability. I asked for help from a friend who has greater skills at writing than me and we have used some artistic licence but in essence this is the conclusion of the story.

I love you.

After the night of my master's death, I lived on the streets of Paradys for a long time. I think I lost my mind. Certainly I lost all sense of time. I lived on scraps and slept wherever I could find shelter. Nothing made sense to me anymore. Nightmares tore my nights apart. The days blurred one into another, a surface of life behind which I knew lay horror. I trusted no-one. I believed my fellow men were all unspeakably evil.

One day, seeking forgiveness and redemption for a desecration in which I had played such an important part, I knocked on the door of a monastery and asked to be taken in as a novice. I demonstrated my skills at reading and writing, and finally I was accepted in the lowest rank, given the lowliest jobs. After several years, I became a novice, and finally I took holy orders to become a monk in the order of St Michel, the archangel.

To my confessor, I explained what had happened. I pressed my face to the ground and wept. I am not sure the priest believed me. I suspect he thought the story was another nightmare, a hallucination from my time of insanity on the streets. Nonetheless, he gave me absolution.

After years had passed, I dared to make enquiries about the fate of the creature I had seen dragged into Paradys and violated so cruelly. I could find out nothing – rumours and whispers only. I pursued my life of contemplation and service. At the age of forty-seven, I became a prior and had the authority to continue my research into the archives of the church and the inquisition.

Finally, thirty years after that midsummer night, I found what I was looking for. I travelled to a monastery in the heart of the city for a meeting with the Abbot of the Order of St Jeanne and I explained what had happened to me, and humbly admitted the part I played as a boy. The Abbot, a bent, elderly man with cataracts over his eyes, covered his face with his hands when I described what had happened.

He took me by the hand, and led me through the cloisters and courtyards of the monastery. It was a closed order – the men who crossed this threshold as monks took a vow of perpetual silence and would never leave. Even after death they remained within these walls – their bones heaped in the caverns deep underground.

I passed several of these silent brothers as the Abbot led me deeper into the labyrinth. They raised their eyes to look at me. Some nodded. One took my hand and kissed it. Did they know who I was?

Outside an arched wooden door, the Abbot halted and asked if I was ready. I crossed myself and nodded. He stepped back and gestured for me to open the door.

I took a deep breath and whispered the Ave Maria. The door was unlocked and swung open easily.

A tiled floor and a window like a wheel of golden glass, with sun streaming through. Paintings on the wall of scenes from the Old Testament, shelves of books, and a vase of daffodils brilliant with colour. A figure was seated at a desk, its back towards me. It seemed to be writing. I could see a quill in its hand. I stepped forward.

Unlike the monks, this figure had long, brown hair. As I approached, the sitter stopped writing and put the quill down. The parchment on the table was illuminated: capitals of gold leaf, fine Latin script, complex and beautiful illustrations of mythical beasts. I had never seen work of such strangeness and beauty.

At last I looked into the face of the writer. It took an effort of will for me to raise my eyes and behold the creature. For so it was. Of course it was; I had known it since stepping into the room. The years had worn away its strangeness and I couldn't see the filmy wings. Dressed in a simple woollen robe, it could have been of either gender, or none. The creature stood up slowly and regarded me. I had changed greatly. Could it recognise me? Had it even seen me clearly on that terrible night? A look passed between us. I sensed it knew.

'Is it time?' The voice was calm and deep.

I nodded. The creature slipped its arm through mine. I hesitated for a moment, but it led me to the door. We walked out, back through the monastery, the corridors and cloisters of stone. Monks stopped as we passed and each time the creature gave a benediction. At last we stood before the great doors. Two monks pulled them open, revealing a view of the city with all its beauty and sin and glamour and chaos. The sun was high and bright. The creature stooped with a sigh and touched a violet pushing its way through a crack in the paving stones.

'What will you do?' I said.

The creature smiled and made the same gesture of benediction over my head. 'I will live.' It stepped away from the monastery and walked out, into the city.

My lover has sent me something else: a colour print-out of a page from an illuminated manuscript. The capitals are gold. The Latin text is fine, and illustrated with arcane pictures of animals (a dormouse, a toad and a stag) as well as a mermaid and a medieval angel carrying a mirror. I cannot read the text but my lover has translated several lines and written them on the back of the page. The last line reads:

I have glimpsed your face in a mirror forged by angels, locked in a windowless room.

Is any of this true? It is now.

Original illustration by Tanith Lee for her novel
Day By Night, 1980

Happily Ensorcelled

Kari Sperring

The first Tanith Lee novel I ever read – indeed, ever owned – was *Quest for the White Witch*. I was 15, and I was drawn to it by the cover, which depicted a woman on her own. I no longer remember where I found it, though it can't have been any of the bookshops near to where I lived then. This was 1978 and US paperbacks were hard to come by, particularly if, like me, you were largely dependent on W. H. Smith. It may have been on the one and only trip I made to the famous science fiction and fantasy bookshop in London, Dark They Were And Golden Eyed. It didn't come from my usual source of sf at that time, the Andromeda Bookshop catalogue: I know that because I remember seeing the cover before I bought it. I didn't know it was a sequel; all I knew was that the cover and the blurb were alluring – lost cities and haunted mountains and that mysterious, fascinating white witch. I fell into the world it described and emerged addicted. This was a writer to love, to seek out and read avidly. It was probably the most influential impulse buy I ever made. I saved up my baby-sitting money, and ordered everything else I could find by her from Andromeda. I lent her books to friends, and spent morning walks to school discussing them with S, who lived just down the road from me. Our favourite back then was *The Birthgrave*, with its complex, conflicted, clever female protagonist.

The following year, Tanith was a guest at Seacon 79 and S was there with her brother. I was deeply envious, but she told me all about it afterwards. Tanith, she told me, looked exactly like one of her heroines, and she was a wonderful, engaging speaker. We were both agreed: Tanith was a sorceress, a person of deep and powerful magic, and we were happily ensorcelled.

I've bought every new book Tanith wrote ever since. Her works take up two complete shelves on one of my bookcases and I read and reread them to this day. She is a touchstone writer, a grand master, a beacon and exemplar of what fiction can be. Her work, for me at least, possesses the resonance and quality of myth, of that deep authentic connection to the subconscious and the antique and the collective human experience. The worlds she created are real; they seem to me to draw from the most powerful parts of the collective unconscious, and her characters are both uniquely themselves and vessels for our oldest archetypes. There are very few writers indeed who can do this and almost none aside from Tanith herself who do it consistently. I don't know how she does it: she was special and talented in ways that most of us will never be. I just know that the stories she wrote are utterly immersive and convincing and true.

Unlike most of the other writers in this anthology, I never had the privilege of knowing her well. I only met her four times. But she was always lovely to me, kind and encouraging and supportive, and being one of her nieces is the highest honour I can imagine. I first met her in 1981, when she came to talk at the university where I was studying. I remember her reading from one of the books in the *Stormlord* sequence and then a parallel passage from a story she'd written as a child, with a dramatic heroine with a mocking laugh and a tendency to throw herself from basement windows. She was, as S had said, a wonderful speaker, engaging and funny and insightful. I don't think I asked any questions: I was too busy listening.

Many years later, at the beginning of my own career as a novelist, I had the privilege of being on a panel with her at Eastercon. It was that old standard, Women in SFF, and my co-panellists included Liz and Sarah and I think, Freda, along with Juliet E McKenna and Tanith. All of us newer writers said the same thing; that we were here, that we were writing as we wrote, what we wrote, because of her. She was in a very real sense the tutelary deity of British fantasy, and particularly of British women fantasy writers. I only ever had one long conversation with her, over dinner at World Fantasy Con in Brighton. We talked about all sorts of things – books and writing and mythology and cats. It's a memory I treasure and I wish I had had more chances to spend time with her. She was incredibly kind about my writing, something which continues to awe me. (The nicest compliment I have ever received was when one of my editors told me that a passage in one of my books reminded her of early Tanith Lee. I can hope!)

Being asked by John and Storm to participate in this anthology is an incredible honour. And being allowed – being *asked* – to write in a background Tanith herself created is astonishing and humbling. Her worlds, her characters feel like they're part of the fabric of my life. (I've read *Don't Bite the Sun* and *Drinking Sapphire Wine* so many times I can practically recite parts of them.) I knew at once which world, which book, I wanted to write about. *Day By Night* isn't one of Tanith's more famous books, and it's not one I hear people mention often. But it has haunted me since I first read it, back when it was published in 1980. That world of dualities and parallels – day side, night side; aristocrats and exploited workers; heat and cold; people who are shadowy mirrors of each other – is an incredibly powerful symbol, somehow. It deals with justice and social class and the need for revolution, all topics which obsess me as a writer. And it has as heroine my favourite of all Tanith's characters, the diffident, troubled, Vel Thaidis Yune Hirz, who in the end acts not because she's particularly brave or heroic but because she must. She's not a kickass heroine, or a magical dream girl, she's a very real young woman and I love her for that.

Back in 2009, on that panel, I told Tanith that I'd always wondered what happened next on that world, after the end of the book. And she said, 'So have I.' This is my suggestion: one possibility as to the consequences of the events of *Day By Night*. It's not the answer to my question: only Tanith herself could answer that. But it's a guess. I hope it's a guess she might have found at least a little bit plausible.

Night in Day

Kari Sperring

'Ivelle, that thing cannot be done.' The voice of the robot was smooth as silk, no snag or crumple breaking through to disturb its composure; no hint of pity or compassion shading the ageless bland surface of its face. Ivelle Yune Zem lowered her eyes to hide the welling of her tears from its empathic regard and turned away without replying. It was, in the end, only a machine. It could not be hurt by either her distress or her departure.

Besides, their exchange was always the same, reduced already by the passage of time to ritual.

Robot, I wish my genetic material and that of my husband mixed in the matrix to make a child.

Ivelle, that thing cannot be done.

She had railed against that, once, weeping and raging into the calm indifference of the machines. *Why not? Why can it not be? You have his genetic print embedded in your memory. Why can you not use it? Why will you not use it? Why will you not heed me, help me, take my pain away?*

The robots had sought to soothe her with scented breezes and soft music, the comforting foods of her nursery days and the hazy embrace of drugs. They had wiped her tears with their cool insensate hands and urged her into her Maram chamber to sink into heavy

137

unhealing sleep. That was as close as they could come to comfort, these human-faced, sweet-voiced unfeeling machines. That was what they were designed to do. They could whisper and placate, lull and drug, but they could never take even the smallest step towards healing her.

They did not even really understand that she was in pain. Machines registered distress only as a problem they must address. Two of them followed her as she drifted away down the pale corridor. It did not matter where her feet took her, within her vast mansion. Each room was as empty as the last. Nothing breathed, aside from her. Nothing ran or smiled or laughed. She was all there was, all there ever would be, since Ermarth had died under the teeth of a lionag and her heart had stopped.

She took a turn at random, partway down the hall, and found herself in one of the many reception rooms that littered the mansion. As was the custom, the bulk of its windows were painted, to create patterns of deep colour across the smooth white floor. But it had amused her husband sometimes to gaze out at the endless baked expanse of desert that bordered the estate. The mansion of Yune Zem stood atop a great escarpment. The cliff side of the house faced inwards, towards the zenith, the centre of the world where everything shrivelled and died under the relentless hammer of the sun. On the opposite side, the rocks sloped downwards more gently and had been laid out by former generations of the Yune Zems as formal gardens. Ivelle walked in them sometimes, her body shielded from the harsh sun by an embroidered canopy held up by her attendant robots. They had not changed since the days of her husband's parents: Ermarth had had no interest in them, and she had found all her interest in him. She could, of course, have instructed the machines at any time to change this element or that, to create a stream to meander across the sweeping lawns, or to cause her vista to blaze with coloured tender plants. The machines would do anything she told them, short of granting her the child – her child, Ermarth's child – that was her one real desire.

She went to the nearest window, the dark polarised inner lids of her eyes lowering to protect her from the glare. Below her, the cliff dropped down, sharp red-brown bones of rock. Its jagged ridges would break her limbs as surely as the lionag had crunched Ermarth's, could she only reach them. The windows were sealed shut: no fresh winds blew across the lands of the Yunea to cool its inhabitants. The air baked along with everything else on this nightless world, and when they came, the desert winds were hot and sand-laden. She laid her hands on the window, felt the outside heat against her palms. Another Jate to pass alone, another waking period to fill with pacing and silence.

'Ivelle, your cousin is here.' This robot spoke in lower tones, programmed thus by Ermarth for variety. Four Jates and three Marams since she had stood by the window to stare out at the desert. Ivelle sighed and raised her head from the embroidery with which she toyed. The one thing she craved even less than her solitude was the company of others of her kind, the aimless princes and princesses of the Yunea. But she laid down her needlework and rose, and followed the robot to the citrine and jade salon where her unwelcome guest waited. The robots had already brought wine and caffea, sweets and spiced patties. Copper-tinted liquid ran over the textured surface of one wall, to plash in a lemon crystal basin. Plants of chrysoprase and beryl shimmered through the liquid sheen. The guest reclined elegantly on an amber couch, toying with a crystal goblet. She looked up as Ivelle entered and smiled a practised sympathetic smile.

'Ivelle. Still so pale and sad.'

Ivelle bent her head to receive her kinswoman's kiss, then took a seat on the edge of a separate couch. Dorlis Yune Ket was not here to console or condole but to observe and plan and calculate. Ten long years since Ermarth died. Ten years in which Ivelle had sunk deeper into her widowhood. Oh, she was still young, as the princes of the Yunea accounted such things, and the Yunea Matrixes could form a child of her genetic heritage at any point, granted an appropriate father. But Ermarth was gone, and Ivelle did not remarry, and the Kets were kin to the Zems.

Dorlis herself had a son and two daughters who must share the Yune Ket estate with cousins of their own. Yune Zem would make a fine home for one or more of them.

Not that she would say so, of course. She would never be so crass. But Ivelle could read the calculations behind her smile.

Now, Dorlis made her routine enquiries about Ivelle's state, and provided all the detail Ivelle did not ask for about herself and her husband and her endless tedious kin. Ivelle nodded and sipped caffea and did not smile. And Dorlis shook her head and sighed over her lethargy. 'You must look after yourself better, my dear. You are the sole heir of the Yune Zems.'

'My household machines will keep me alive.'

'But what a life...' Dorlis hesitated, perhaps seeing some glimmer of resistance on Ivelle's face. She leant forward. 'But I almost forgot. A scandal, my dear. And once again it's Yune Hirz.'

Ivelle did not want to know. It would do no good to say so. Dorlis was convinced that she needed to be shaken out of her chosen lethargy, and thought such means as this would work. She stared down at her lap and said nothing, letting Dorlis' voice wash over her. Perhaps she should sympathise. Yune Hirz, like Yune Zem, was haunted by tragedies. The murderous girl Vel Thaidis, on whose fate she had been forced to help pronounce. The tragic death on a hunt of Ceedres Yune Thar-Hirz, so reminiscent of Ermarth's. Now, doubtless, the last scion of the family, Velday Yune Hirz, had likewise come to some painful early end. She turned her cup in her hands, watching the dark liquid swirl and sway. Dorlis rattled on, something about Velday – so he was not, in fact, dead – bringing his Slumopolis mistress to live with him in his palace – 'In his mother's own rooms, too, my dear. They say she's remodelling the palace in the worst possible taste. All mirrors and diamonds, can you imagine. And she just some slum child who can barely write her own name. My husband called on Velday a while ago – something about hunting – and the girl was there with him. Not serving the guests, even, but sitting with them, bold as you wish.' Dorlis paused for breath and, it appeared, recharging, disposing of a sweet pastry in three bites and then washing it down with a long draught from her goblet. A hovering robot refilled it.

'And the Yune Onds held a J'ara party, and, would you credit it, Velday took the girl with him! I wouldn't have known where to put myself. It's one thing to indulge these creatures in the Slumopolis, but in respectable houses....' Dorlis hesitated again, seeming to require some response.

Ivelle made a non-committal murmur into her caffea. She could sense Dorlis' eyes upon her, burning disapproval.

Dorlis continued, 'But that's just the start of it. There's more. My dear, they have a child.'

Ivelle's head snapped up. Despite the caffea, her mouth was suddenly dry. Blood pounded at her temples. A child... Yune Hirz had a child. Through stiff lips, she said, 'The Matrix permitted...?' It could not be possible. The machines of Yune Zem would not permit the mingling of her essence with the recorded traces of her late husband. How, then, could the machines of Yune Hirz create a child from the imprints of Velday Yune Hirz and some nameless young woman born in the Slumopolis, without known pedigree or rank?

Dorlis set her goblet down on the fragrant carved table that stood beside her couch, and reached out to pat Ivelle's hand. 'My poor child. I know that was your dream.'

Ivelle said nothing. Her hand stung, under that soft, leech-like touch.

Dorlis stroked her fingers for several long moments before sitting back and taking up the goblet again. 'It wasn't the Matrix. The girl bore a natural child. Can you imagine? Why Velday permitted it, I cannot think. But he did, and now he has gifted Yune Hirz with the offspring of this creature. It won't be recognised, of course; how could it be? A natural child to be a prince of the Yunea! The slum girl has probably passed along all sorts of defects. They say...' and Dorlis lowered her voice, even though there were only the robots to overhear, 'they say it was born a monster. Poor Velday. Poor, poor Velday.'

Jates and Marams passed. Ivelle lost count of them, each so alike their predecessor. She walked her halls, and stared out at the desert, added new pointless stitches to her embroidery and let the robots weave silk flowers into her hair. All was as it had been before Dorlis' most recent visit, as it had been since Ermarth died. And yet, and yet... The tale of the Yune Hirz child haunted her, shadowing her footsteps, ghosting through her nights. She did not dream. Or, if she did, she did not choose to remember. But hour by hour, Jate on Jate, she remembered and pondered and seethed. At last, one Jate, her restless feet led her to the Yune Zem library, where she pored over book after book, trying to make sense of what had happened, to her, to Ermarth, to Velday and his slum girl. This, this accident of chance for Yune Hirz, who neither deserved nor needed it. For her, nothing. Perhaps she should send a robot to the Slumopolis and order it to bring back for her some male, with whom she could mingle herself. That was allowed. But her flesh shrank from it, shrank from anyone who was not Ermarth. She had promised his memory, on that sharp burning day when his shamefaced companions – Yune Ond, Yune Thar, Yune Chure – had brought his ragged body back to her, spread out across his bloodied chariot. Not one of them had had the courage to speak the news, nor even to look her in the eye. They had left that to the hunting robots, battered blood-stained things tearing her world apart with their fluted words in Courteous Address. She had screamed and raged at them, begged her household machines to heal his wounds, make him breathe and walk and speak again. And the aristocrats of the Yunea had clustered round, their faces blank and frozen. Two of them had stayed with her that Maram: Omevia Yune Ond and another girl; Ivelle could not remember who. They had wanted to hold her hands and stroke her hair, as if she were the heroine in some sentimental Slumopolis play. She had run from them, tried to break into the sealed chamber where the machines prepared her husband's body for appropriate disposal. Her hands had been bruised for Jates afterwards, their polished almond nails worn to bleeding stubs. And through it all the sweet relentless robot voices denying her, and the twittering idiocies of her fellow princesses who could not, could never, understand.

She had wanted to kill herself, then, wanted to hurl herself from the height of the cliff so that her body might be as mangled as Ermarth's. But the great windows were impervious to her assaults and the palace locked its outer doors against her.

Ivelle, it is not permitted.

She did not know Velday Yune Hirz, not well. He had been less than twenty when Ermarth died. She had not known his unfortunate sister. They were half a generation younger than her, acquaintances met only at the largest gatherings. And then, the Yune Hirz estate did not lie close to hers: several other domains separated them. And yet, that Jate, somehow, Ivelle put off her desert-coloured mourning garb and dressed herself in elegant greens and ambers; instructed her personal robots to strip the dull burnt earth colour from her hair and re-tint it in softest jade. She was not done mourning, she would never be done mourning, her heart was numbed for all time. But she might not, should not, wear her mourning openly into a house that welcomed new life. She ordered her aircraft to be readied. Not Ermarth's hunting vehicle. That was long gone, dismantled in the earliest hours of her grief. This was a slender elegant thing in silver and gilt, with filigree wings and bright-hued glazed insets designed solely to cast pretty patterns across the comfortable interior. She had one of her attendant robots drive and commanded two others to attend her with cool drinks and fans. Sweet music played to distract her. She had instructed the driver-box to keep to the desert, skirting the more sculpted parts of the estates over which she passed. If her vehicle were to be seen, to be recognised... Under the canopy, she sat tense and fretting in her cushioned seat, while the robots sought to soothe her jangled muscles with gentle massage and to distract her with books and sweets. Hours passed and she remained silent and still. Under her silks and gauze, her heart fluttered in her chest. To do this thing, to attempt this thing... Again and again, her lips trembled as the words that would command the aircraft to return to Yune Zem hovered there and fled. She would not dare to try this a second time. If she turned back, she condemned herself finally to slow death by loneliness.

Perhaps she slept. Her mind was caught in a fever of fear and anticipation, blurring the passage of time. When the craft slowed to a halt, she started, clutching at the arms of her chair. 'Ivelle, we have reached the palace of Yune Hirz,' one of the robots announced, and she nodded. She had only been here once before, summoned to join the heads of all the other clans to pronounce sentence on Vel Thaidis the murderer, the lost. That meeting was a blur in her memory. She might have been anywhere, sentencing anyone. She could recall nothing of the domain, let alone the accused.

It lacked but a few minutes to the fifteenth hour. She would be keeping J'ara, whether she wished it or not. The aircraft came into land on a smooth expanse of coloured gravel, bordered by tall feathery plants. The mansion was but a short distance away, along a broad footpath, shaded by more of the slender plants and accompanied by a pretty watercourse. Yet a small chariot, drawn by a single mechanical anteline, waited, lest the guest not wish to walk. The aircraft folded its wings and unfurled a shallow stair: Ivelle's attendant robots hovered ready to steady her should she slip or fall. At its foot, a machine belonging to the Yune Hirz waited, holding up a great green sunshade. 'Welcome, Ivelle Yune Zem.'

Ivelle turned her head to look at it, in the fashion of Courteous Address. 'Is Velday Yune Hirz at home?'

'He is. He awaits you within.'

Ivelle let the robot escort her to the chariot. Her attendants followed, skimming over the gravel. They passed moss-green lawns and tall succulent trees. In the distance, a lake shimmered. The great front doors to the palace were open, and Velday Yune Hirz stood on the threshold to greet her. He inclined his head to her as the robots handed her from the chariot. He looked... How could she read his expression, she who barely knew him? And yet though his face was smooth, it seemed to her that he looked drawn, strained as he stood there in his fine garb smiling his polished social smile.

He said, 'Ivelle Yune Zem. I confess I did not expect you.'

Was there a faint stress on the final word? Ivelle rather thought there was. 'Forgive me. I should have sent word I wished to visit.'

'You would have been unique if you had.' This time

146

the note of strain was clear.

Ivelle realised, finally, the extent of Dorlis' spite. They would all have come, the bored and aimless princes and princesses of the Yunea, hungry for novelty. They would all have come to gape and ogle at that most unlikely thing, a natural child born to one of their own. To one of their own by his Slumopolis mistress.

She looked down at her gilt-sandaled feet. She said, 'I should not have come. I... I wanted to help.' She began to turn away, back to the chariot. She was a fool, falling into Dorlis' trap.

His voice arrested her. 'Wait. You've travelled far. Let me offer you refreshments, at least, before you go.'

She hesitated.

Velday added, 'You're the first person who's apologised. That's a lot, right now.'

Something made her turn back. The smoothness was gone from his face, and it now showed open stress. He was still very young. So easy to forget that, when every aristocrat was in such a hurry to be adult and jaded. Young, and, like her, alone, save for the girl from the slum. She said, 'Thank you,' and let him escort her inside. She had been here no more than a handful of times, and, for all Dorlis' comments, she could see no sign that much had changed at all. Certainly, there were no diamonds, and no more mirrors than one might expect. The air was cool and limpid, heat scrubbed from it by the house machinery. From somewhere drifted the sound of a chame, smoothly played. She said, 'Will your... Will your companion be joining us?'

Velday looked at her for long silent moments, his eyes searching her face as if he would read her thoughts. Well, and she had nothing to hide. Nothing that would harm him, anyway. She let her eyes meet his and held his gaze. Perhaps she passed his scrutiny. He turned to the nearest house robot and said, 'Ask Tilaia to join us.'

'Yes, Velday.' The robot glided off.

Ivelle inclined her head towards the direction of the music. 'She plays well.'

'She's smart. She learns quickly.'

Ermarth had been intelligent, restless, always looking for some new form of entertainment, of occupation. Ivelle said, 'An interest in learning is a good thing.'

'Yes. I wonder sometimes...' Velday broke off as they entered a pretty salon, painted to seem as though the inhabitants found themselves in some exotic impossible underwater world. Shifting patterns of green and grey and blue flowed down the windows, so that the sunlight seemed to ripple as it filtered into the room. Mechanical fish swam in a curving central basin: its wide brim served as a table. Chairs made to resemble fantastical shells, and lined in pale pink and lilac silk clustered in intimate groups. Quiet robots set platters and jugs within easy reach, then retreated. Velday waited until she was seated, then inspected the jugs. 'Would you care for caffea, or something cool? There are fruit juices of several kinds, or I can send for wine.'

Another piece of Dorlis' gossip, that: Velday Yune Hirz loved his wines and drugs too much. Ivelle said, 'Juice, please. I don't mind what kind,' and he handed her a goblet. She sipped it in uncomfortable silence, watching the fish wiggle their way about the pool. What was she doing here? What had she been thinking? Her hands clasped tightly about the goblet, lest they betray her by shaking. The music had stopped. She heard footsteps approaching, marked out by a sweet jingle of bells.

'You summoned me, my prince?' A sting in the voice, though the tone was sweet. The young woman who entered the room was slightly built and slender, with bones made to carry beauty. Her hair was a soft fall of bronze; her face exquisite. She was dressed in better taste than Dorlis managed most of the time. But her eyes were angry and she tapped one bejewelled, belled foot on the floor.

Velday rose. 'We have a guest, Taia.'

'I'm not blind.' The girl swung to stare at Ivelle. 'Another one come to see the monster, no doubt? Another high-born lady come to be entertained.'

'Taia...' Velday began.

Ivelle cut him off. Setting down her goblet, she stood. The girl was half a head shorter than she, or more, and her small frame showed the marks of childhood hunger. Ivelle said, 'Zenena Tilaia, I came to see you, I... I know what it is to be lonely in a palace.'

Tilaia stared at her for several instants. Then she started to laugh, throwing her head back. 'Lonely, princess? I admit that's a good one. Thinking to soften me up with your kind words. But I'm not lonely, I assure you.' She twined one arm around Velday's, rubbed her cheek against his shoulder. 'How could I be lonely, with the patronage of my prince?'

'I was married,' Ivelle said steadily, 'and I loved my husband dearly. Yet sometimes I was lonely even when he was alive. He loved to hunt, to drink, and I did not.'

'I think you're lonely,' Tilaia said. 'I think you're lonely and you seek to amuse yourself by patronising me.' Velday tried to free himself from her clasp and she held him tighter.

'I'm lonely, yes,' Ivelle said. 'But I don't look to you to

cure that. I just...' She did not know how to talk to this woman, this façade of stone and hostility. She inhaled, finished, 'I wanted to help. My cousin came to me with spiteful gossip, and I... I wanted to help.'

'You help me, princess? And how might you do that?'

'I don't know,' Ivelle admitted. 'But I thought... I thought perhaps we might become friends.'

Ivelle had read of hysteria: she had never before seen it. A robot came to her, led her from the salon to an adjacent chamber, serving her with food and wine, while somewhere nearby Tilaia laughed and screamed and descended into wrenching loud sobs. The books in the Yune Zem library had told her about natural childbirth in all its brutal fleshiness. They had detailed the ills it could bring in its wake, from haemorrhages to blood-poisoning to soul-churning depression. And she had remembered the days after Ermarth's death and her own desolation. Those feelings, she knew intimately. Dorlis would sneer, no doubt, to see her here waiting on the will of a girl from a J'ara house, but Ivelle ate the food and sipped the wine, and, when the robot indicated, allowed it to take her to a comfortable Maram chamber. She slept well, without dreams, and rose clear-headed and calm. Robots served her fruit and caffea; one brought a message from Velday. *Forgive me for my neglect of you, and thank you for remaining. I hope to be able to attend on you later this Jate.* Ivelle nodded, and thanked the machine. 'Thank your lord for his hospitality and tell him I am happy to wait on his convenience.' She did not have her embroidery here, but there were books and music, and gardens to roam that were new to her. Her own robots hovered at her back as she wandered them, enjoying the change of vista. The Jate passed and Velday did not come. But nor did he send her a request to leave. She retired again to the Maram chamber and slept.

The chamber was designed to filter out sounds as well as light, but something woke her at around the fourth hour. She rose from her couch and cracked open the door. Somewhere below her, robots were moving. Something had dropped or been thrown. Ivelle found a satin wrap to wind over her sleeping robe and padded barefoot towards the source of the disturbance. A thin strand of music led her from her guest quarters towards another wing of the palace. The music – oh, how well she knew those mindless, repetitive soothing tones! – grew louder, brought her at last to corridor decorated in bronze and umber and green. A squat house machine busied itself cleaning liquid from the floor; a knot of humanoid robots hovered by a part-opened door. Several held jugs or bowls or vials. Ivelle cast an eye over the contents, settled on a flask of the renowned Hirz wine. Taking it from the robot's unresisting grasp, she straightened her shoulders and laid a hand on the door. To the robots, she said, 'You may go.'

They were not hers to command. But her voice carried the authority of generations and class, and perhaps even they were strained by the situation that pertained in this house. They hovered a moment longer, then, one by one, retreated down the corridor.

Ivelle went into the room. Another Maram chamber, but there was precious little rest inside. Cushions and silk coverlets strewed the floor; the air was misted with soporifics. Tilaia lay supine on the bed, her face hidden in her arms. The useless music blanketed the air. Ivelle said, sharply, 'Turn that off. And scrub this air. No-one could sleep in this fug.' The tune stopped in mid-phrase; a faint breeze began to blow, clearing the mist. Ivelle looked around her. An empty goblet lay on its side by the bed; another stood on a low shelf. She gathered both, sniffed them. Neither had held anything more sinister than juice. She wiped them with the edge of her wrap, then poured wine into both of them. Tilaia had not moved. Ivelle was certain, for all that, that the girl was well aware of her presence.

She set one goblet where the girl could reach it, then sat down on the edge of the bed and took a sip from the other. She said, 'After my husband died, my house seemed to decide it could bully me. Drugs in my food, in my drink. Robots offering rote comfort. Soft melodies everywhere I went, until I was ready to scream. Though if I did, there were more drugs and more music. We're not supposed to *feel*, you see. It's inelegant. We're supposed to be bright and brittle and... and convenient. I expect it's far worse in the Slumopolis. I imagine no-one can afford to be unhappy or afraid, not where they can be seen.' Tilaia did not respond, but somehow Ivelle knew she was listening. 'I expect it's far worse than I could ever begin to imagine. But I do know about the feelings, the despair and the hurt and the anger.' She took another sip. 'Especially the anger. I loved my husband very much, but I was so angry with him for dying when he didn't need to. We don't need to hunt lionag. We don't need to take risks like that.'

'Send your princes to live in the slum, if they want to know risk.' The words were muffled, but there was no hostility to them.

Ivelle said, 'Perhaps that might be better. Perhaps that might make them kinder, too.' She considered the girl.

She could be little more than twenty. 'I think Velday means to be kind, but I suspect he's afraid of your anger. Did he tell the robots to tend to you?'

A nod.

'He's hiding, I suppose. I wonder if that's why he had me stay, so he wasn't alone with you? My robots tried to make me send for my distant cousins. I didn't let them, though. They would have made it worse.'

Tilaia rolled over. Stripped of make-up, her face was stark in its beauty. Her eyes were dry. She said, 'And you? Are you making things worse, now?'

'I don't know,' Ivelle said. Part of her marvelled at her cool. Where did it come from, this sudden courage? 'But I know the drugs don't help. Or the lullabies and pillows.'

'It's a monster.' Tilaia's voice was a whisper. 'I thought... I thought it meant something, that I could bear a child. It doesn't happen in the J'ara houses. We... They feed us something. And in the Slum. But it happened and I thought... I thought...'

She'd thought Velday would marry her, at a guess. Ivelle did not know what held those two together, but it did not look like love. Or not just love. Ivelle said, 'I don't believe Velday intends to abandon you.' She barely knew him. But he did not seem to her to share the cruelty that so many of his kind possessed. 'Do you want me to ask him?'

Tilaia stared at her and Ivelle realised she had finally surprised the girl. She came from a world in which one might not so simply ask. Ivelle continued, 'And, you know, if he does turn you out, you may come to me.'

'I don't do women.'

'I don't do anyone.'

Tilaia sat up and reached for her cup. She gulped

down a good half of its contents, still staring at Ivelle. Then she said, 'What do you want?' She eyes narrowed. 'Is it the child? I told you, it's a monster. The other princes and princesses came to see it, and they screamed or looked sick. Shall I show it to you and make you scream, too?'

'Doesn't your son or daughter have a name?'

'No. Velday...' Tilaia's lip trembled, and she bit it, hard. 'Velday wanted to give it one, but it's only going to die. There's no point. They die in the slum, natural births. And this one is a monster. Of course it's a monster. What else could it be, given who gave birth to it? A slum girl mated to a prince!' She gave a short, painful laugh. 'Any goodness or health was burnt out of me long ago. Or rubbed away, by my first prince. He was a monster, too, but he didn't look like one. This one... It's clear. You'll see. She raised her voice. 'Robot? I know you're still out there. Fetch the monster.' Tilaia drained her cup and poured out another. Her eyes were still fixed on Ivelle's. Somehow Ivelle knew it was important that she withstood that gaze.

'Tilaia, I have brought your daughter.' The modulated tones of a nursery robot. Tilaia turned away at last. Ivelle swallowed. The robot entered the chamber, a satin-swathed bundle in her arms. 'Tilaia, do you wish to hold her?'

'No.' Tilaia's voice was harsh. 'Unwrap it and show it to Princess Zem.' She turned to face the wall, shoulders rigid. The robot rotated and held out its arms to show Ivelle.

A child. A baby, eyes screwed up shut in sleep, underlip protruding. Her hair was black, a thick shock framing the perfect little head. Her body, her tiny limbs, were flawless.

Her skin was white, like the underbelly fur of an anteline. Under the pitiless sun, she would blister and burn in minutes. Ivelle put out a shaking hand to touch the perfect cheek. She said, 'You will have to take extra care in covering her.' She had never heard of such a thing. Her own skin, like Tilaia's, like Velday's, was the colour of burnt gold. She went on, 'But she's lovely.'

'You didn't scream.' There was a note of wonder in Tilaia's voice. Ivelle looked round and found the girl watching her. 'Why didn't you scream?'

'Why would I?' Ivelle caressed the cheek again. 'I don't want to wake her. '

'It's hideous. Every time the nurse takes it near light, it screams. It's foul and broken, just like me.'

'Her skin is too fair. The sunlight must hurt her.' Under Ivelle's fingers, the child's skin was soft. 'She's perfect. Beautiful.'

'It's a punishment on me, on Velday, because...because...' Tilaia's voice began to fracture.

Ivelle caressed the baby's cheek one last time, then turned. She said, 'You're frightened. I understand that.'

'You can't.' Tilaia's hand tightened on the goblet. 'How could you? You don't know what we did.' Her voice rose. Ivelle fought an urge to step back.

The robot said, 'Tilaia, shall I take the child back to her nursery?'

'Take it anywhere you want! Throw her from a cliff, leave her in the desert, I don't care.'

'Tilaia, I cannot do that.'

Quietly, Ivelle said, 'Take her to the nursery.' The robot turned and slid silently away.

'And you get out, too!' Tilaia raised the goblet,

threatening. 'Go! Get out! I don't want you. I don't want anyone.'

The goblet bounced off the door as it closed behind Ivelle.

Another Jate passed, and another Maram. The robots of Yune Hirz escorted her to bathing rooms and salons, played music for her, brought her meals and drinks. When she walked in the gardens, they identified for her those plants she did not recognise. Her personal robots styled her hair and held up her sunshade. Twice, she began her preparations to leave. Twice, a robot came to her with a message. 'Please remain a little longer, Princess Zem.'

She saw neither Tilaia nor Velday. But when she asked a robot to show her to the nursery, it took her there at once. The nursery robots let her hold the child and help to feed her. In this cool shady room, the baby was calm and peaceful, spending much of her time sleeping. Awake, she watched with round eyes the pretty toys the robots hung over her cradle, and curled her tiny hands around Ivelle's finger. She still did not have a name: Ivelle asked.

It was not uncommon for children to be raised with little contact with their parents, at least in the palaces of the princes. Ivelle could barely recall her own mother, who had drifted through her early years like some bejewelled mythical being. After all, women no longer bore children within their bodies; men no longer watched them wax with new life. The matrices that created heirs for the aristocracy were tucked away, doing their work in quiet seclusion. It was much the same in the Slumopolis, where children were created as needed then released to fend for themselves once they could talk and walk and feed themselves well enough. Most of them died. She had cried over that when first she heard; in the early days of her widowhood she had woven plans to go to the slum and sweep up the smallest to nurture. Yet somehow, she had never followed her plan through, afraid to be alone in that harsh and pitiless place. She suspected that should she attempt it, the lawguards, the unfeeling machines that watched both palaces and slum, would somehow prevent her.

But this child, this small pale fragment, had not been formed in a matrix: Tilaia had carried her the way women used to, long eons ago. Surely that should make a difference? Ivelle could not understand the mother's horror. The child's tender skin could be shielded from the sun until the household machines worked out a way to heal it, and otherwise she was healthy and strong. *It's a punishment on me and Velday. You don't know what we've done.* Ivelle did not believe there were gods, and, lacking gods, how could there be punishment? Perhaps Tilaia's deprived upbringing in the slum had led to some weakness in her that had affected the child, but that was hereditary and not punishment, and no-one's fault. The medical robots would solve it, as they solved all the ills – all the physical ills – of the nobility.

She asked the robots how long she had been at Yune Hirz, counted on her fingers and wondered how she had lost track of time. Within her own dwelling, hours and Jates weighed heavily on her, dragged their feet, empty and pointless. Here, they fled from her on pale wings, while she rocked and sang to and smiled at the baby. It was the Jate after that – or the one after, or the one after – that Velday finally sought her out in the nursery. The robot nurse was bathing the child, and Ivelle watched and waved toys to entertain her. She did not hear Velday enter: she started when he spoke from behind her. 'Tilaia was a natural birth herself, you know. She has a brother, a twin. Perhaps that's why...' He stood at her shoulder: Ivelle twisted to look at him. He went on, 'In the Slumopolis, people are employed to look after the children grown in the Matrices, rather than robots. Perhaps I should find a way to pay you.'

'I like to do it.' Ivelle dangled her hand in the aqua, making ripples in the green surface to amuse the child. 'I like your daughter.' Awake, the baby looked much like any other, with her dark hair and dark eyes with their inner lids. Only her skin marked her.

'Tilaia is superstitious. She thinks the child is cursed.'

'Why? Because her mother was born in the slum?'

'No.' Velday's tone was pensive. 'Are you religious, Ivelle Yune Zem?'

'No.' The question was unexpected. Ivelle turned properly and studied him. He looked.... He looked conflicted.

He said, 'So you no longer visit the temples?'

The gods and their mechanical priests had been no good to her when Ermarth died. They had been little good before that. She said, again, 'No.'

'And you've never been in the upper room of any temple?'

'No.'

He said, 'Come with me. I mean, please.' He offered her an arm, a curious out-dated gesture. Ivelle rose, drying her hands on the soft towel a robot offered her, and let him lead her from the room. He said, 'I've decided to trust you. You came, and... I suppose I need to tell someone.'

They descended a wide stair, went through a door that let out onto a long jewelled gallery, with views over the lake and the gardens. Velday said, 'Tilaia believes the child is mis-made because of some fault in herself, because she comes from the slum. Either that, or we're cursed, because we killed someone. At least, we made sure he died.'

'Was this in the Slumopolis?' Ivelle could not imagine it could be otherwise. The death of a prince or princess was momentous, the news travelling swiftly from estate to estate, discussed by all who heard it. It was an event, a happening, in a world that was all too predictable.

'No.' Velday came to a halt before one of the windows. Its sepia tint cast a grey sheen over his golden skin. 'We killed my friend. Ceedres Yune Thar. My so-called friend. I had trusted him, loved him, and he betrayed me, betrayed my sister...'

Ceedres Yune Thar had died on a hunt, like Ermarth. Just like Ermarth. Dorlis had made sure Ivelle heard all the details of that, watching her face greedily for every drop of pain. She said, 'That was a lionag. A hunt...'

'Yes. But he meant that death for me, and I... I tricked him. Tilaia procured me a drug and I gave it to him. Then I let the lionag take him. He wanted my sister and she refused him, so he trapped her, had her exiled, humiliated. Afterwards... I wanted to find her, but she fled. She died. They told me she died.'

Ivelle remembered Ceedres Yune Thar. A great, golden, laughing man who smiled and jested and fostered drunkenness and decadence and, somehow, corruption. He had not been one of Ermarth's intimates: he had been some forty years Ermarth's junior. She had always been glad of that. She had felt nothing at his death, save horror and pain at the means of it. She said, '*If he did those things, if he threatened you, then you were right to kill him.*'

Velday laughed, once, without mirth. 'Yes. But Taia... Since the child, it eats at her.' He looked down at her. 'I want to ask you something, Ivelle. I want to ask you something huge and unreasonable.'

Her mouth was abruptly dry. Her hands, by contrast, were clammy. She rubbed her palms against her skirt. She said, 'What, then?'

He gazed at her in silence for several moments. Then he said, 'It's the child. Tilaia wants to send her away, to the slum. But that would kill her. So I thought, I wondered.... Ivelle, would you take her? You seem to care for her. And perhaps if she isn't here, if Tilaia doesn't have to see her, or hear about her, she can heal.' He stopped. 'She can't be my heir. I don't think she can. She's not properly Yune Hirz. I asked the house lawguard. But she can live here, on the estate, any estate. There's no law about that. Perhaps she won't live long. They don't, you know, the people in the Slumopolis. But she could have some kind of life, somewhere, maybe...' The words trailed away. His gaze held Ivelle's and she saw that he was shaking.

The child could not be her heir, either. She could never be the child Ivelle might have had with Ermarth. But she lived and she was in need. Ivelle said, 'Yes. Yes of course I will. But there is one thing...'

His brows drew together. 'If you feel you must report me to the lawguard, please leave Tilaia out of it.'

'What?' She had all but forgotten his confession already, wrapped in the news of the child. And then, '*No, not that. It's just... She needs a name, your daughter. You need to give her a name.'

'Oh.' From the surprise in his face, it was clear he had not thought of that aspect at all. 'I don't really... I mean, I haven't thought, since she was born...'

'And before?' She and Ermarth had looked to have long years together before asking the house Matrix to mix them an heir, but they had sometimes played with the idea anyway, *I want her to have your eyes, your bone structure. I want him to have your courage and your kindness.*

'Teja,' Velday said. 'Call her Teja.'

Ivelle ordered her aircraft to lower the shutters on all its windows for the journey home. The child Teja slumbered peacefully in the cushioned familiar embrace of her nursery robot, while Ivelle tapped her instructions for the palace into the machines located in the arms of her own chair. By the time they landed, a covered walkway had been erected between the landing pad and the nearest entrance, and every window in the mansion had been double-tinted to reduce the sun's glare to the minimum. The rooms adjacent to Ivelle's own had been outfitted as day and night nurseries, though she also ordered a cradle to be placed in her personal Maram chamber, next to her couch. The scions of princes might be raised at arms' length, but this child – *her* child – would be kept as close to her as her own skin, sheltered and tended and nurtured like the rarest plant. In those last minutes of her sojourn at Hirz, the centre of her world had shifted and she had been made anew. The mourning garments were banished from her closet, to be replaced with bright silks and satins that would catch the child's eye. She had her robots bind bells and ribbons into her hair, for Teja to catch in her chubby hands. Her waking hours were spent singing to the baby, feeding her, bathing her, selecting music for her playtimes and sleep times, choosing stories to be recited by the robot nurse, or played out in vivid images on the pearly walls. Sometimes, Ivelle even read to the child herself, bending over the screen like one of the pictures in the most old-fashioned books. The medical machines advised her on appropriate nutrition, on exercise and development and activities. Jate on Jate, year on year, Teja grew, straight and slim and quick-minded. Her eyes behind their dark inner lids had the same tilt as Tilaia's; the angle of her cheekbones, the shape of her chin bespoke her mother also. But the strength of her limbs, her height and health bore testament to her Hirz ancestry and the care of Ivelle. In all but name, she was a princess of the Yunea.

She learnt quickly, racing through her lessons well ahead of others of her age (or so the educational machines assured Ivelle). That was all to the good, for, aside from Ivelle, she had no human companions. The princes and princesses of the Yunea came to gawp, as they had at Yune Hirz, and left with false smiles over muttered comments about the ill effects of grief. Dorlis at first offered syrupy affection and smooth, unkind words of advice. Ivelle endured the first and ignored the latter. 'Such a funny creature you are, my dear. Such whims! But you know these creatures – endearing as they can be – don't live as long as us. You will break your heart all over again, you know, if you get too attached to one.'

'She's a child, Dorlis, not a creature.'

'Of course, of course,' and Dorlis patted her cheek. But her eyes were calculating, and Ivelle was not fooled. After her cousin left, she summoned a medical robot and instructed it to make a full assessment of her sanity.

'That is not needed at this time, Ivelle. You show no signs of distress or illness.'

'Nevertheless, I wish it. And I wish it repeated twice a year.' Better to be prepared: the bulk of her peers might dismiss her behaviour as eccentric, but Dorlis did not forget her family connections and was greedy for her sons. Perhaps, in time, Yune Zem would descend to one of them, if Ivelle did not choose to remarry. But remarriage no longer seemed as impossible as it once had. Her palace was once more a place of warmth and happiness.

At least, Ivelle was happy. She believed – she hoped – Teja was as well. She was a serious child, preferring books to games and, once she reached seven or eight, prone to long silences and long stillnesses. Ivelle and the palace provided everything she might need, save companionship of her own age, and she did not seem to miss it, as far as Ivelle could judge. Nor, once she was past her toddler years, was she a particularly affectionate child. She discussed her lessons with Ivelle, presented her sometimes with carefully painted pictures of the gardens, read her way through the library, or gazed zenith-wards towards the desert beyond the cliff, through the tinted windows, a self-contained cool presence within the bright walls.

She knew Ivelle was not her mother and that her true mother lived elsewhere. It did not seem to trouble her: she asked few questions about her parents and seemed content enough. There were no visits from Tilaia, no messages. Velday came once or twice when she was small, bearing toys and making awkward conversation. But faced with the child, he proved tongue-tied and once she was old enough to converse his visits ended. The gifts continued, intermittently. Teja received them with polite pleasure and composed suitable messages of thanks for the robots to transmit to him.

She seldom left the palace. Though the palace machines wove her garments that shielded her tender flesh, and the medical robots blended lotions that protected her skin, no long-term solution could be found for her pallor. Exposed to the sun, she blistered: the sun was the only thing she hated or feared. Yune Zem became a place of deep shadows and cool darkness, decorated in purples and blues and greys. 'How exotic, my dear!' said Dorlis, but later on Ivelle overheard her describe the palace to another as 'Just one big Maram chamber, you know. So unhealthy. So morbid. And how will the girl ever learn her place, with Ivelle pandering to her so?'

That was at a gathering at Yune Ond, which Ivelle was obliged by rank and tradition to attend. She was used to Dorlis' closet spite – and the more overt repulsed curiosity of some of the others of her peers. And yet... Teja was nine years old and all she knew was the palace of Yune Zem. She knew nothing of the slum from which her mother came, or the conditions there: remembering Tilaia's superstitious fears, Ivelle had instructed the education machines to tell the girl only the most basic facts of the Slumopolis. *A monster. What else could it be, given who gave birth to it? A slum girl mated to a prince! Any goodness or health was burnt out of me long ago.* But Teja was no monster. Towards the end of her ninth year, Ivelle kissed her good night, instructed the robots to take good care of her, and ordered a chariot readied. If the aristocrats of the Yunea were determined to see the slum in her child, then she would arm herself with the knowledge she needed to defend her. She sent a message to Yune Hirz, too, asking certain questions, and instructed the machines of the house to transmit it to her attendants, wherever she was. She was three-quarters of the way to the slum before any answer reached her, and it was brief. Well, the machines that ran the slum kept records, as they did everywhere: she could still find out what she needed, it would merely take a little longer.

Women of her class seldom went to the Slumopolis, and never alone. Even the princes usually went mainly to hold J'ara, and spent their time in the ornate houses devoted to their entertainment that ringed the true slum. Ivelle had visited one once, with her husband, to see a dancer whose talent had been widely praised amongst his friends. The girl had been all they said and more, a strange fragile creature who used her body to convey emotions that seemed wrenched from her core. Ivelle had wept to see her pain and showered her with compliments and gifts of jewelled bangles. But the transformation in the girl – from true artist to fawning, cringing flatterer – had shocked and repelled her and she had asked Ermarth to take her home. She had never been to the inner part of the slum, where the majority of its inhabitants struggled to wrench a living from the pitiless soil and the corrupt businesses that it grew. She had never seen more than the public rooms of one of the more respectable J'ara houses.

She instructed the driver robot to take her to the Instation closest to the boundary of her estate, at Tenth Hour Hest-Ne. The great electronic barrier that ringed the inside of the estates parted to let her pass without hesitation. The lands beyond were flat and scorched, scored by great metal roads and sub-divided into vast crop fields where human men and women, rather than robots, laboured ceaselessly to force what sustenance they could from the dry earth. The Slum itself stood at the centre, on the highest – the hottest – point, which was useless for anything else. The Instation marked its rim, a blocky ugly building of dust-pitted metal, pierced by spindly towers that snatched signals from the air and transmitted them on to lawguards and the vast governing machines that kept the inhabitants in check. No robot servitors here, save for a very favoured few. Machines enforced the laws, controlled water rations and access to shelter, monitored jobs and ensured that the human population knew its place. There was no room here for beauty or leisure, only endless toil and struggle to survive. The sun, almost directly overhead, was merciless, snatching every drop of moisture from skin and hair. There was no shade, save what the utilitarian buildings could provide in their cramped and mean interiors. There was no liquid, save the scant amounts dispensed from public cisterns. There was no mercy. Ivelle shivered under the canopy of her chariot, and almost – almost – turned back. But this was for the child, not for her. This was necessary. She instructed the chariot to halt at the gate of the Instation, and allowed her attendant robots – four of them, all armed with the hunting weapons of her class – to hand her down from the vehicle. One of the opened a shade over her as she walked the short distance to the door. It was closed, blank, featureless save for a small grille. She hesitated, uncertain. One of her robots said, 'Shall I announce you, Ivelle?'

'Yes. Please.'

'The Princess Zem requires to speak with the keeper of this Instation.' The robots invariably used Courteous Address with Ivelle: she had not known they could speak any other way. There was a long silence, then the door slid open to reveal a plain corridor. A man stood in the centre of it. He was short and thin, dressed in a shapeless grey tunic, decorated with haphazard lines of thin braid. His dark scalp showed through the thin strands of his hair. His face... Ivelle realised she stared, looked away. She had never seen such a face before, skin pulled tight to the bones, carved with deep lines and mottled with the scars of too much sunlight. This, then, was age unmitigated by care or medical attention. She swallowed, said, 'Excuse me, Zenen, for coming upon you unannounced. I am Ivelle Yune Zem.'

'Welcome, Princess.' Was there a note of mockery in his voice? Ivelle was not sure. He swept her a low bow, then indicated the corridor. 'This is a rare honour: I am, of course, at your service. Would you perhaps care for wine? Aqua? Please, enter. My quarters are humble, but they are, of course, fully at your disposal.' He indicated that she should come inside. Ivelle hesitated again, reminded herself of the protection her robots gave her, then followed the man into the building. He led her to a small room, windowless and lit by painful white light set into its dull grey ceiling. A screen and several buttoned panels were arranged beside a desk made out of a single piece of brownish plastum. Benches and a couple of plastum chairs faced it. There were no paintings, no cushions, nothing that was not plain and functional.

The man dusted off the seat of one chair with the sleeve of his tunic. 'Sit, princess.'

She sat, while he keyed a sequence into one of the panels, which slid open with a hum to reveal a bottle of some yellowish fluid and two lumpy glasses.

He poured a portion of the liquid into both glasses and

handed her one. His hand, brushing hers in passing, was dry, callused. She held the glass in nerveless fingers. This must be the infamous wine of the Slumopolis, which the younger aristocrats took pride in consuming in great quantities on their visits here. Would her host be offended if she did not taste it? It seemed all too likely. He had moved the second chair to face her, and sat down, drinking deep from his own cup. His smile revealed crooked yellow teeth. Two were missing at the front. Ivelle reminded herself a second time not to stare and took a sip of the wine. Sharp, thin, like under-ripe fruit. She forced herself to keep her expression bland.

He said, 'Does the wine please you, Princess Zem?'

'It is unique,' Ivelle said.

He smiled again. 'That it is. Nowhere can match the flavours we create in Slumopolis.'

She said, 'I am in search of certain information. I need to find someone. A man. A man who lives here.'

'I am the sole resident at this Instation, princess. Are you, perhaps, searching for me?' This time, the insolence was clear. His gaze passed over her, slow and appreciative.

Her hand tightened on the glass. 'Certainly, to meet with the keeper of this station was my first goal, but the particular man I seek is someone else.' She needed this man to help her. She did not think simply commanding him would do her much good, even with her robots present. She smiled in return, added, 'Regrettably.'

Doubtless he saw through her. But he looked at her attendants and nodded. 'I am, of course, delighted to be of help. A man, you say. What is his name?'

'I don't know.' That had been the burden of her message to Yune Hirz. But Velday had been absent, and

Tilaia would not speak to her. She went on, 'There's a girl, a woman, who used to work in a J'ara house. Her name is Tilaia. She has a brother.'

'There are many J'ara girls and former J'ara girls, princess. Some of them have brothers.'

'This one... She was a natural birth, a twin. She was the mistress of Ceedres Yune Thar and then... and then of one of his friends, who took her to live in his palace.'

'The princes of Yune Thar seldom visited this district, princess, even before they fell. Now, there are none to visit us at all.'

Ivelle handed the glass to one of her robots and made to rise. 'Then perhaps I should enquire at a different Instation.'

The man held up a hand. 'But natural births are rare. And recorded. I can look through our records for twins. But it will take time and resources...' His voice trailed away.

He wanted payment. She had prepared herself to that. She held out a hand to another of her robots and it produced a silk bag from one of its compartments. She opened it and took out a small handful of tech credits. 'I understand. Would this, perhaps, compensate you for taking you away from your duties?' She held them out.

He hesitated a moment, looking again at the robots, then bowed. 'Of course, princess.'

She slipped half the credits back into the bag, held out the remainder. 'A down-payment. Now, how long will this take?'

'Without names it's harder, of course, but...' He was still looking at the robots. At their weapons. 'Perhaps a third of an hour, princess.'

'Then I'll wait.' She sat back in the chair and took the

glass back from her robot. 'Please, do not feel obliged to entertain me.'

She barely recognised herself in this calm control. Perhaps something of Ermarth's courage had remained behind to aid her. Or perhaps it was the thought of her serious, beloved Teja, who deserved to know everything about what she was, and why she was special and precious to Ivelle. She sipped the bitter wine and looked about the featureless room, while the man turned to his screen and began to tap away at the keys and buttons. All about her, the building hummed; low, grinding, metallic. She took care not to mark the passage of time in any way, instead accepting a feathery fan from one of her attendants and a book from another. Ermarth would be proud of her, if he did not first think she had run mad. She did not jump when, at last, the man spoke. 'I have found him for you, princess.'

'Excellent.' She rose, and indicated to a robot that it should pay the man the rest of the agreed sum. 'Please transmit the information to one of my attendants. And thank you for your time, Zenen. You do not need to escort me out: I have taken up too much of your valuable time already.'

The brother's name was Sherner and he lived in a surprisingly spacious dwelling in the district of First Hour hest-uma, in the same area as the J'ara houses and homes of the upperlings who profited from them. His source of income was unclear, at least from the material the keeper had provided, but Ivelle suspected Tilaia's hand at work. Or, more likely, Velday's. A robot servant met her at the door, and took her to a large, gaudy salon, painted in bright colours with fanciful scenes of imaginary palaces. It stank of cheap perfume and wine. She was seated on an over-cushioned couch and served sticky sweets and yet another goblet of the sour wine, this time sweetened with teaspoons of sugar. 'The Zenen will be with you immediately,' the robot said in a fluting voice, and glided away, doubtless to resume some other job of work within the building.

Sherner was not what she expected. Somehow, she had been picturing him as a male version of Tilaia. But Tilaia was beautiful, and this man was… not. Like the keeper of the Instation, his frame showed the marks of childhood privation, but he was not precisely thin. His skin showed pale marks, old scars mixed with newer stretch marks as he put on flesh. His eyes were narrow and deep-set. His hair had been dyed a raw reddish orange. In place of a tunic, he was well dressed in draped shirt and leggings, also in lurid colours. His teeth were brown. He stared at her boldly for long moments, then said, 'Well, you're not what I expected.'

Had Tilaia contacted him? Ivelle's mouth was suddenly dry. Her lips felt dense and stiff. He continued, 'A princess, my servant said. I assumed you must have come from one of the J'ara houses, looking for a favour. But you're too plainly dressed for that. A real princess, then. I'm honoured.'

He did not sound honoured. He did not trouble to use Courteous Address. Ivelle swallowed, made herself speak. 'I… My name is Ivelle Yune Zem. I… I know your sister.'

'Do you?' He looked her up and down, and took his time over it. 'Let me guess, she's attracted your man, and you want me to stop her? Sorry, I can't do that. As you see,' and he waved a hand at the room, 'she and her prince make it worth my while not to interfere with her. Or him.'

Blackmail, then, or something like. Perhaps Sherner had some inkling of Velday's plot against Yune Thar. Or perhaps he simply knew how to make himself unpleasant enough – and inconvenient enough – for Velday to find it useful to pay him off. He would not, Ivelle realised, be intimidated by her robots, even armed. She should not have come here.

He resumed talking. 'I doubt Taia sent you here. She has no use for me. So it's something she's done. Or said.'

This man was Teja's uncle. The thought was horrifying: she wanted him nowhere near her precious girl. And yet... Ivelle drew in a long, shaky breath, and said, 'It's neither. I... I have come to tell you about your niece.'

He barked out a great shouting laugh, throwing his head back. 'My niece? You mean Prince Hirz's bastard, I take it. I thought it died. Or he exposed it, like the runt of a dogga litter.'

'She... she lives with me. She doesn't know about you, or... or her family. And I thought....'

'You thought I might like to come and visit her, yes? Stay in your pretty palace and drink syrups and listen to fancy music? Or do you just have a taste for men who are... rather more rough-edged than your princes? You can scratch that itch easy enough at any of the J'ara houses. Or at one of the markets, if you really like it raw.'

'No. I...' She wanted to rise, she wanted to run from the room, from the slum, take refuge in her familiar comforting mansion. She was fixed on the couch as if bound with metal bands. 'I just wanted Teja to... to know about her mother's birthplace.'

'Taia wiped the last trace of this place off her pretty feet the day Yune Hirz took her in, and good riddance. She'd laugh, if she could see you here. And she'd be right. Your Teja's better off never knowing anything about the slum or anyone in it. And you...' and he took a step towards her, 'you'd be better off never coming back here. Princess.' He clapped his hands, and the robot servant glided back into the room. He said, 'The princess is leaving now. See her out. And, if she comes back, don't open the door to her.'

The light seared her eyes. Perhaps, after her years in her shaded palace with Teja, she too had lost her resistance to the sun. She ordered the chariot to close its canopy and darken its windows, and leant back in her seat, letting her outer lids fall. Under her veils and wraps, her skin stung. The movement of the chariot cooled the air around her: she drew deep lungfuls, gulping it down as if she had been starved of oxygen for the last several hours. Was this how Teja felt, when she ventured out of the palace into the grounds, under the stern lash of the sun? Her head ached: she rubbed at her temples, and one of her robots, attuned to every change in her, began to massage her shoulders. She said, 'Stop!', for once failing to use Courteous Address. It was a machine. It could not be offended. And anyway, it belonged to her.

She went straight to her Maram chamber, on arriving at the palace, omitting her usual enquiries after Teja. She was not ready, yet, to face the child, to try to explain to her about the other half of her origin. Once ensconced in her sanctum, she ordered soft music and drinks sweetened with fruit and drugged to help her sleep. The silken pillows felt rough against her cheek, as if her visit

173

to the slum had burned her defences away. *Your Teja's better off never knowing anything about the slum or anyone in it.* Perhaps that was true. Yet Dorlis and others would never allow Teja truly to belong amongst the mansion estates, either. Ivelle turned over, searching for a softer place, a cooler place, an answer. She would, most likely, outlive Teja: she was older than the child by some forty years, but she was the product of a palace Matrix, not a natural birth, and her genes had been selected and scrutinised for the best possible combinations. Teja carried Tilaia's hereditary alongside Velday's, and Tilaia was a random product of the slum. Ivelle turned again. Say she outlived Teja: that meant she could supply the girl with every comfort she needed for all of her life, every luxury. Everything save companionship – but Teja seemed hardly to crave the latter. Perhaps there were some among the princes who were less snobbish than Dorlis, and would deign to befriend her, later on. Or perhaps she might seek suitable children from the nurseries of the Slumopolis and raise them also.

You'd be better off never coming back here. Princess.

She did not want to go back to the Slumopolis. She did not want to face the heat and the cruelty. She did not want to know…. Neither the keeper nor Sherner had been amongst the most wretched who dwelled there, and yet their faces and bodies were marked by privation. The people she had seen working the fields had been stunted and twisted, aged by sun and toil. She did not want to think about this. She wanted to forget. She should think of Ermarth, tall and handsome, laughing as he spun her round in a spontaneous dance. She should think of Ermarth…

She fell asleep at last and dreamed of her husband,

bloodied and torn, his face marred by lines of age, staggering on failing legs from clump to clump of desiccated grain, trying to harvest it with a blunt and rusty knife. His hands were twisted, fingers thickened: they fumbled on the knife handle, letting half the grain fall. His skin was dry and cracking. And above him, the sun burned on and on, without end.

Heat woke her, a hot blast of air on her skin. She opened her eyes, blinking, to find the door to her chamber open and Teja standing just inside it, watching her. Ivelle sat up, made herself smile. 'Good morning, dear one. Did I oversleep?'

'No.' Teja, as ever, was serious. Her eyes fixed on Ivelle's face. 'I wanted to know where you'd been. You didn't leave a message for me.'

'I didn't? I'm sorry about that. I must have been pre-occupied. But it was nothing, really. Just... Just an estate matter. An inspection.'

'The house told me you went to Slumopolis. But it was Jate. And you don't keep J'ara.' Teja hesitated, then added, 'You're too old. And too dull. Dorlis says so. I heard her.'

Ivelle had not thought to instruct the house to keep her destination from the child. She had not thought Teja would think to ask. Normally, she showed little interest in what Ivelle did. She said, 'It was still an inspection, of sorts. There was something I wanted to learn about. And Dorlis says a lot of things. You know that.'

'Yes.' Teja continued to stare at her. There was nothing of Velday in that gaze. Precious little, too, of Tilaia. The directness – the coolness – reminded Ivelle uncomfortably of Sherner.

175

She said, 'What did you do, yesterday?'

'Studied. As usual. And Dorlis came, and ate cakes, and told me I needed better manners if I expected ever to be welcomed at any of the other palaces. She thinks I'm insolent.'

A warm glow of anger woke in Ivelle. 'Dorlis has no right to make any comment at all on your behaviour. It's no concern of hers. Your manners are far better than either of her sons'. And if she mistakes intelligence for insolence, then she's even more foolish than I thought.'

Teja shrugged. She was, it appeared, no longer interested in Dorlis. She said, 'You're tired.'

'A little. It's all right.'

'And you were crying. I can see that.'

'I had… I had a bad dream.'

'Oh.' Teja was not interested in dreams. She turned to leave. On the threshold, she halted, and looked back over her shoulder. 'You'll never be my real mother, you know, even if you go to Slumopolis. Whatever you do.' Her expression was oddly calm, level; the calculating face of an adult rather than a nine-year-old girl.

Ivelle swallowed. 'Did… Did Dorlis say that to you?'

'Dorlis? No. I thought it for myself.' And Teja turned again and left.

Ivelle dropped back against her pillows. The headache was back. The panel near her head, the one that monitored her sleep and adjusted the chamber as needed, began to hum, a low buzz of concern.

She said, 'I want another sleeping draught. And tell the house… Tell the house to have the educators teach Teja every last detail about the slum.'

The education machines, obedient, added the history and

anthropology of the Slumopolis to what they taught Teja. Sometimes, self-flagellating, Ivelle made herself sit in on the lessons, listen, learn alongside the girl. Teja, the good child, listened and asked only the right questions. Ivelle, not so much.

Why don't the people of the Slumopolis use machinery in their fields?

They do not have such machines, Ivelle. There are not sufficient resources for that. And if the fields were worked by machines, there would be no work for the people. They would starve. They would have no shelter. They would have no access to water.

Later, alone, Ivelle said to the house, 'The aristocracy, the princes and princesses... We don't work in the fields nor labour in factories. Yet we have food and water and shelter. And more.'

'You are the lords of this world, Ivelle. You are not required to labour.'

'But if we aren't, why can't the slum-dwellers also be provided for? Cared for?'

'They have water rations and cubicles to rent. They have access to some medical attention.'

'But they work. They... they suffer.'

'There are not enough resources to provide also for all of them, Ivelle.'

'If I sent some of my robots...'

'There are more workers than you can replace, Ivelle. More than the resources of Yune Zem can support.'

Time passed. Between Ivelle and her beloved Teja nothing changed. Ivelle told herself nothing changed. Teja herself seemed unmoved by her new knowledge of the conditions of the Slum. She continued to prefer her books, her walks, her hours contemplating the desert. She no longer painted pictures for Ivelle, that was true, but instead, as she aged and grew, she began to converse, asking Ivelle about this book of classic literature and that, about the music she studied and the art of poetry. She was a perfect child of the princely houses, accomplished and graceful. It was Ivelle who lay awake, Maram after Maram, fretting over what she had seen in the slum. It was Ivelle who diverted such machines and credits as the house could spare to ease the burden of those fieldworkers who laboured in the district closest to Yune Zem.

They were not grateful. They took the credits, used and damaged the machines. But Ivelle did not want gratitude. She did not think she wanted gratitude. She wanted... She did not know. But she had the machines repaired and sent back, made economies in the upkeep of her estate, and her own pleasures. Her peers began to call her *eccentric* rather than *grieving*: their false sympathy and greedy curiosity turned into mockery and distrust. 'My dear,' said Dorlis, creamily satisfied, 'you will never remarry and make an heir, going on like this.'

'Perhaps,' said Ivelle, her mind already elsewhere.

And the years went by. A handful of the youngest princes and princesses began to call, at first curious to see the strange slum girl who lived amongst them. Some smiled behind their hands and never returned. Others – including Dorlis' younger son – came back. The salons of the lower palace began once again to fill with laughter and music. Teja, wrapped in silken veils and sheltered from the sun by her robots, began to take aircraft to this estate and that, to attend parties and gatherings.

She never went to the slum. And Ivelle... Ivelle never returned there.

'Every time I see you, my dear, you look worse.' Dorlis leant back against the cushions and took a sip of her sweetened caffea. 'Fatigued, dull, thin. I told you adopting that slum child would only lead to trouble.'

'I'm quite well,' Ivelle said, 'and Teja is no trouble at all. Rather the opposite.'

'Hmm.' *I don't believe you,* said Dorlis' tone. But outwardly, she merely smiled and reached for another little cake. 'Then perhaps it's the light in here. Yune Zem is so gloomy these days.'

'The sunlight hurts Teja's skin,' Ivelle said.

'Of course.' And Dorlis changed the subject to gossip about the large Yune Ond family.

Ivelle sat back in her seat, trying to ease the ache in her neck surreptitiously. She would never admit it to Dorlis, but lately she never felt really well. Headaches, pain in her shoulders and neck, a heaviness that affected her limbs. Her head felt heavy, somehow clogged, as if her synapses were filling slowly with some thick viscous fluid. Perhaps she should have the house medical machines examine her. Long ago, she had read, people used to slow down as they grew older. It still happened in the slum. But her kind lived long, healthy, youth-filled lives. She was tired, that was all. She had not been sleeping well recently. She would speak to her robots and have them adjust her Maram routines.

Dorlis was twittering about a Yune Ond daughter who was enjoying a liaison with one of the Yune Ket cousins, and how *suitable* it was. 'Not at all like Casten.' And she set down her goblet and glared at Ivelle. 'Really, Ivelle, I expect better of you.'

Casten was Dorlis' younger son. Ivelle remembered him as a slender boy, prone to satirical remarks and a rather languid pose. He was not amongst the youngsters who had embraced Teja. She said, 'I'm afraid I don't..?'

'Your fosterling!' The word was a curse. 'Young people will have their playthings. I accept that. J'ara girls and boys, hunting, pavra... But in their place. Not... not to the exclusion of everything else.'

'I regret,' Ivelle said, stiffly, 'that I have no idea what you might mean. Casten is not a friend of Teja's. If he has run into trouble, it has nothing to do with her.'

She expected Dorlis to scream at her, or else rise and sweep out, all rigid outrage. But instead, Dorlis leaned forward, a curious smile on her lips, and said, 'So it's true. You don't know. Tell me, my dear, when did you last see your dear child?'

This Jate. The words rose to Ivelle's lips and stopped there. No, not this Jate. The house had been empty, silent save for the hum of machines and her small noises. She had not asked the robots where Teja was. She frowned. 'I believe...' When had it been? Not last Jate, but the one before that? Longer ago? Teja did not keep J'ara in the slum, of that she was sure, but she and her friends sometimes stayed overnight in each other's houses. They were a serious crowd, interested in music and dance and poetry, rather than the pleasures of hunting and drinking and drugs. Teja had said... Ivelle's brain would not function. Her head was heavy. She turned to the nearest robot, and asked it, 'Where was it Teja said she was going?'

'The Zenena Teja said she was going to Yune Tu, Ivelle, to examine their library. It contains unusual texts that she wished to examine.'

Relief washed over Ivelle in a cool wave. She met Dorlis' gaze. 'Teja is studying at Yune Tu. She and Lledri

Yune Tu share an interest in antique plays and poetry.'

Now, she remembered. Teja smiling at her in the dim light of the morning salon, her words tripping over one another in excitement, as she described the book which Lledri had uncovered in her family's vast and neglected archives. *'It hasn't been performed for two hundred years. Maybe more. We're going to read it together, and maybe even put on a performance ourselves.'*

Ivelle smiled at her visitor. 'I'm sure you'll agree that's harmless.'

Dorlis snorted. 'That's what she *said*, is it?' She rose. 'Lledri Yune Tu has gone with the Yune Onds to watch a dance performance in the Slumopolis. My elder son is with them. Casten is not. Nor is your Teja. I suggest you put a closer watch on that girl, Ivelle. I suggest you wake up from whatever malaise it is you've let yourself fall into, and find exactly what it is you've brought into your home.'

Dorlis was spiteful. She lived to gossip and interfere, to judge and manipulate and harm. So Lledri had gone to watch some dancers. It was probable that Teja, who cared little for that art form, had remained at Yune Tu to study the newly found play. She would be back this Maram or perhaps the one after. So Ivelle told herself as she paced the corridors, trying to think through the miasma that clogged her head. Dorlis was just trying to make trouble. Doubtless, Casten had made the mistake of expressing some kind of admiration of Teja in his mother's hearing, and she was anxious not to let it go any further. Which only went to show Dorlis' foolishness: Teja could have no interest in that aimless, trivial young man. Teja would be home later, full of her discoveries and her plans for the stage performance. Perhaps she could hold it here at Yune Zem. The green salon could be used as a theatre, it was big enough. Ermarth's grandmother used to hold musical recitals there, according to the stories his father had told. Teja would like that. And it would be good to have guests again, life and joy filling the dim rooms.

Ivelle reached the end of the passage and took a turn at random. She would have the house research the food and drink preferences of the age in which this playwright had lived, and offer Teja's guests a feast to match their entertainment. Perhaps they could wear the garments of that age, too. Her plans occupied her as she paced, along another hallway, up one of the gilded stairs, through the line of linked salons where Ermarth's parents used to entertain. She and Ermarth had preferred the other wing, looking out over the gardens, but Ermarth's mother, like Teja, had liked to gaze out over the desert. Teja might not be a Yune Zem by birth, but she had grown up with their memories all around her. She had as much right to be here as any other of the family. Ivelle should have the house research the laws of inheritance, too. Somewhere there must be a means whereby she could declare her darling girl her heir. She stopped, and realised that her feet had brought her to the rooms Teja had taken over as her own: she had moved out of the suite next to Ivelle's when she was fifteen or so.

Ivelle had been here before, of course. Teja often invited her, to share meals or listen to music. But she made a point of waiting to be invited. Teja was a young woman now, and entitled to privacy. But her wanderings had brought her half-way into the suite before she realised. She hesitated, began to turn to go. She must remember to apologise to Teja later for her inadvertent intrusion.

It was just... There was something not quite right, something that tugged at the edge of her consciousness. She became aware that her palms were sweating. Perhaps Dorlis was right; perhaps she was unwell, or at least a little run-down. She rubbed her hands on her skirt. Something odd, something disquieting... She swallowed. Casten Yune Ket was a profligate user of the fashionable drugs of the Yunea. If Dorlis were somehow right, if Teja had been spending time with him, he might have introduced her to some of the less savoury ones.

Anxiety drove respect from Ivelle's mind. She summoned robots, ordered them to search the rooms, looking for anything that did not match with Teja's usual habits. She herself searched the girl's Maram chamber. Cushions, books, and, in a small carved box beside the couch, a collection of phials, which she did not recognise. She took the box out into the largest salon. 'House, what are these?'

One of the robots came over to examine the contents, using its slender fingers to test the contents. 'These are Slumopolis drugs, Ivelle. They induce sleep and lethargy.'

Teja did not go to the slum. And her behaviour... She was serious, yes, but she was by no means apathetic. Ivelle said, 'How are these used? How does Teja use them?' The house monitored everything, saw everything.

'She does not use them on herself, Ivelle.'

'Then how does she use them?'

The robot whirred. If a machine could be uncomfortable, it was. Impatient, Ivelle said, 'Tell me.'

'Teja gave instructions you should not be told, Ivelle.'

'I am head of Yune Zem. My orders supersede hers.'

It whirred again, talking to the great machines that ran the house. Then, 'Yes, Ivelle. Zenena Teja gave instructions that these drugs be added to your food and drink.'

Ivelle sank to her knees. The floor in this room was carpeted in silk, finely woven and richly patterned. Her hands dug into the soft pile. She whispered, 'Why?'

'I do not know, Ivelle.'

'And where... where is she now?'

'Zenena Teja has gone in the aircraft of Casten Yune Ket to the former estate of Yune Thar, Ivelle.'

Yune Thar. That name was cursed, these days. Once, it had been a mighty domain, to match Yune Zem and all the other princely holdings. No longer. Slowly, over a century or so, the machines that sustained it had started to fail. No robot servants, no gardens, no fountains and attendants, nothing now save the great shell of an empty palace. The last heir, the last Yune Thar had been a scandal in himself. Golden, laughing Ceedres Yune Thar, beloved of all the young princes. Ceedres Yune Thar, who had been the best friend of Velday Yune Hirz, and, according to Dorlis, Tilaia's original patron. Ceedres, who Velday's sister Vel Thaidis had been accused of wanting to kill, and whose death Velday claimed he had himself encompassed. Ceedres, whose name and lineage were no longer spoken of by any of the princes. Ceedres, who like Ermarth, had died under the claws and teeth of a lionag.

Ivelle rose as if in a dream, and walked to the medical suite. There, she instructed the machines to cleanse her of all the drugs in her system. She dressed herself with care, black trousers, long black tunic, no jewellery, no decoration. Her robots stripped the pale blue from her hair, returned it to its natural dark brown shade. She wrapped a black veil over her head and shoulders and ordered her aircraft to take her to Yune Thar.

Black, the colour of war. But she did not arm herself, nor did she take any of her attendant robots. If she went to war, it was against her own foolishness. She had done something wrong, somewhere in these recent years. She had failed Teja in some way, and she must make amends.

The desert had taken back Yune Thar, dust filling the channels and basins where once aqua had flowed. The house reared up at its centre, a vast reddish-brown hulk, its windows muddied, its doors gaping open. Inside, the air was thick, hot, cloying. Footmarks tracked through the dirty floor: more than one person had come here recently, and more than once. Spine straight, Ivelle followed them through the empty rooms with their skeletal, broken furnishings and fittings.

Teja awaited her in what was once the grandest salon, a great echoing cavern of a room with an empty fountain at its centre. Casten Yune Ket lolled on a shabby couch, his head thrown back, eyes dark with parva. A second man stood at Teja's shoulder. Thin, and reeking of cheap perfume. Several others, men and women, gathered behind, all dressed in the plain garments of the slum.

'Ivelle,' Teja said, 'dearest foster mother. This is an unexpected pleasure. You know my uncle, of course. My *real* kinsmen. And these,' and she gestured to her companions, 'these are my friends. My real friends, not the fools you offered me.'

Ivelle's mouth was dry. It had not occurred to her that she would need to bring water with her into the house. She licked her lips, said, 'Teja...'

Teja held up a hand. 'He told me the truth, my uncle

Sherner. He told me what you kept from me. Oh, you made me study the Slumopolis, of course you did. You had to be sure I knew *my place.* But the rest... My murderous parents, who threw me away and cheated me of my inheritance. Who gave me to you as a toy, knowing all the while that that idiot –' a gesture towards Casten,'– would inherit your estate, and me along with it. Velday and Tilaia killed the last prince of Thar with poison, and Sherner got it for them. They never faced trial. They never faced any consequences at all. My mother,' and she sneered, 'my mother abandoned her brother and her companions to live in a palace.'

'It seems to me,' Ivelle said, 'that Velday made sure your uncle had robots and credits.'

'In a hovel. Like everyone else of our kind. You – all the princes – you live in luxury you've done nothing to earn.

'Yes,' Ivelle said. 'I... It's resources. The house said...'

'Resources.' Teja snorted. 'Why should you have them? Why should Velday? Why not me, or Sherner or any of our friends? We have this,' – another gesture, this time encompassing the room. 'We have this ruin. But why not Yune Hirz, too? Velday fathered me, after all. Why not Yune Zem?'

'I was going to instruct the house, look into the laws...' Ivelle began. Her voice shook. She should not have come here.

Teja held out a hand, and Sherner handed her something. A knife, long-bladed, unadorned, a practical weapon honed on the hard streets of the slum. She smiled, and her smile was not hers, not Tilaia's, but the mocking cold smile that had once been that of Ceedres Yune Thar.

She said, 'There are more of us than you. I think it's time we had everything, don't you?'

Half a world away, where the sun faded into endless grey twilight, a smooth dome rose from the rock. Dere-nentem-dere, Deneder, built by those who shaped and ruled this world, to enable their games. Under the dome, inside one of its buildings, two beings watched Teja advance on Ivelle through a great gold-edged screen. Temal and Ceedres, puppet masters, schemers, heartless genii of this world. They had set these events in motion years ago: the fall of Thar, the expulsion of Vel Thaidis, the revenge of Velday. And complementary events on the planet's second night-bound side, where the people had skins as pale as Teja's. All done for their own amusement, all done to provide them with opponents against whom to play the game. Away around the rim of the world stood the second dome, a second set of controlling screens. Home, that dome, now, to Vel Thaidis Yune Thar, and her nightside companion, Casrus Klarn. They had sought, those two soft-hearted humans, to instil kindness and equity to their world, to reduce aristocratic privilege and ease the lives of those who worked and struggled and starved.

They had played, and Ceedres and Temal had woven their own wishes into the game. A girl born of a woman who Ceedres had once owned, a girl touched by his cruelty. A girl to bring the princes down in blood and flame.

Did she weep, Vel Thaidis, under the other dome, as Ivelle's bright blood made patterns on the soiled floor? Did he curse, Casrus, who dreamed of peaceful revolution? They might never know for certain, but they could suppose, and in that supposition find new entertainment.

And then they could start the game anew.

Tanith Lee:
An Inspiration to a Generation of Female Writers

Sam Stone

When I was first asked to write a story in the world of
Tanith Lee, by her husband John Kaiine, my first thought
was: How could I possibly be worthy? How could I do
any of it justice?

Tanith Lee was one of those writers I came across in
my teens when I first read her short fiction in Interzone. I
was by then already interested in writing and the
magazine represented everything I aspired to do. Tanith's
stories stood out to me. They were emotive and evocative.
The language she used was literary and incredibly
intelligent. I had to learn more about her.

Combing my local bookstore I found a copy of *Sabella,
or The Blood Stone*, and after digesting this magnificent,
sensual and exciting science fiction vampire story I made
it something of a mission to find more of her works. I
discovered *The Silver Metal Lover*. After that I was
completely hooked on her work. Sadly, at the time, it was
very difficult to find full sets of books in a series in
bookstores and libraries and so the offering was sparse: a
problem that resolved itself with the rise of online

bookstores. This was probably how I came across *Vivia* and *Biting the Sun* for the first time.

Some years later, when I'd had the audacity to write my own vampire novel, *Killing Kiss*, I met Tanith at a literary convention called EasterCon. This was in 2008. I had the good fortune to be placed on a panel with her. My daughter Linzi, who had already discovered her works in my paperback collections on my bookshelf, had digested all that was on offer, and was a huge fan of hers as well and she came with me to the convention: she was 15 at the time.

After the panel, Tanith turned to me and said she would love to read my book as I'd mentioned it during the discussion. I nearly fell to the floor with a cry of 'I'm not worthy'. And I knew I wasn't. But I did give her a copy, expecting her to not really have time to read it, and thinking that she had only asked to be polite. However I spent a lot of time with her and her husband John Kaiine that weekend, and we became great friends. By the end of the convention we had exchanged addresses and phone numbers and we were planning to keep in touch.

A few months later, when a major life change happened and my first marriage came to an end, Tanith was a great confidante and friend to me during that time. I was even now looking back at our email exchanges and thinking about what an important time it was in my life to have such a lovely friend. She and I enjoyed frequent long phone conversations, and consolidated a friendship that I felt was always going to be there. She also hugely surprised me with how very supportive she was about my writing. There was never any edge to her about other writers and their works. I even received a beautiful letter from her talking about the book I'd given her, telling me how much she liked it and she kindly gave me a quote to put on the cover too. And – I greatly appreciated things that were inaccurate in the book that she also pointed out. I still have the email with these comments – and believe me I took her advice and corrected those issues for the new edition.

Over the years I've met other writers, dealt with their significant insecurities, but Tanith never seemed to have those. She was lovely to everyone. Supportive, appreciative and very generous with her time and advice for new writers. I wish we could all take a leaf out of her book on that score. I also saw her as a hugely kind person and I know that she has inspired many of my female friends in exactly the same way.

Even when I didn't often see her, her influence spread to the way I approach my work ethic. Tanith gave great advice and one of the things that has stayed with me is that she believed a writer should trust themselves first and that they had to be happy with what they had written above all else. She was right of course: we have to have an enduring self belief in order to continue doing what we feel is the best way to tell our stories. Others will criticise, advise and recommend change. But you have to be comfortable with all of that or you lose something of the raw talent you bring to your work.

When we finally met again some years ago at World Horror Con in Brighton, I was thrilled with the way she greeted me and spent time with me. It seemed that whenever we met, or spoke on the phone, it didn't matter how much time had passed, it always felt as though we could pick up where we last left things. She was always my friend and I never felt that she was false at any point. She cared about me as she did other friends she took to her heart.

When I started working with Telos Publishing, and editing their Moonrise fiction imprint, I wanted to work with Tanith. As soon as everything was set up and running smoothly, I contacted and asked if we might, in our very humble way, be able to republish *The Silver Metal Lover*, or any other of her wonderful titles that she may have available. Tanith came back and gave us an impressive and comprehensive vampire story collection, containing several new, previously unpublished stories, which she wanted to call *Blood 20*. She also offered us a crime novel called *Death of the Day*.

Obviously we were delighted, and I was thrilled to be able to work with her on a professional level. She was a total delight professionally as well as personally. Always helpful, always hard working, and despite the illness that was already taking hold of her, working to deadline.

We arranged that she would launch *Blood 20* at EasterCon (Dyprosium) in 2015, which felt almost as though I had come full circle as this was the event where we'd met initially, and we planned to catch up properly there.

I was looking forward to seeing her again more than I can say. Unfortunately when the time came, Tanith, sadly, was not well enough to attend. David and I were, however, delighted to see Tanith's husband, John, who came along to represent her at the event.

We had known for some time that Tanith was seriously ill, but I had kept hoping for some miracle that would save her in the eleventh hour and keep her amazing talent longer in this world. John has been a rock throughout, and despite the pain he was feeling, managed to remain energetic and entertaining at the convention. So when he emailed me to explain that Tanith had passed away and was no longer in pain: there was both an outpouring of sorrow tinged with a bitter happiness that her suffering was over. And absolutely the deepest regret that we hadn't managed to meet for one last time.

Some people come into your life for very special reasons. I know that Tanith Lee touched many lives, and that she brought them, through her literature (and for those who were fortunate to meet her and know her, however briefly in a personal way) a great deal of joy.

I firmly believe that Tanith was a huge inspiration to many other up and coming female writers like myself over the years, and I feel fortunate that she saw something in me that made me worthy of her friendship and to be considered one of her nieces.

Always missed.

Sabellae

Sam Stone

When he wakes he remembers the smell of her. A rich musky scent. Pheromones that promise heaven. Metallic. Dark. As melodious as her voice.

He remembers when he first saw her. Her face was turned away, but he could make out the aquiline nose, outlined by the veil of black hair that fell down, covering her cheekbones. And then when she turned, eyes meeting his, the colour was overshadowed by the clear jewel at her throat. Was it a diamond? Or merely crystal? It doesn't matter: it is part of her. As life-giving as the breath that heaves in her chest.

He hadn't been on Novo Mars long and found the terra-formed plant life air alien. The people were different too. They had found religion; everywhere he goes he sees images of God. Revivalists they call themselves. It is mythology to him: as ancient as the faith of the Greeks and Romans. Millennia devotion that no one in the present took seriously on Earth. But the Martians did. Oh, not the Martians of old either. They worshipped their own Gods. These are nothing more than settlers, though generations have passed since the first of them arrived. They aren't Earthlings any more than they are Martians.

They are Novo Martians.

She is one of them.

He remembers.

She was sitting on a bench when he noticed her. It was a park not dissimilar to those created on his own world. Trees, though gnarled, twisted as though bearing the pain of their birth from this drier soil. Deformed they were, but still recognisable, and weighted down with fruit.

It was a lemon tree that she hid beneath.

The sun was high in the stark sky, and yet she pulled heavy black clothing around herself as though she was afraid to catch a chill. He noticed the shiver, the fearful glance at the sunshadow that crawled towards her shelter. How she edged back as far as she could into the darkness.

'Can I help you?' he asked.

She glanced up, then quickly back down – *painfully shy*, he assumed. He had found it endearing.

'I need a cab. Quickly,' she said.

'Are you sick? Perhaps I could take you to ...'

'No. Not sick. I just need to find ... shelter.'

'I'll get you a cab ...' he said.

On his return her perfume was all that remained. He waited in the shadow under the tree for an hour or more. She didn't return.

At his hotel he walked into the lift; smelt that musky aroma, and then *saw* her. The doors closed before he could react. At the next floor, he left the lift, ran back down the stairs into the lobby. Tortured by the thought of missing her again – though he didn't know why. She is no one, a fleeting connection. But it was enough to begin a lifelong obsession.

The lobby was empty. Outside the sun burnt at its hottest. Somehow he knew she was not outside.

Later, as darkness fell and the sun dropped below Novo Mars' horizon, he rolled in bed. Fever tortured. Heart burning.

He remembered her. Vivid. Vibrant. Vivacious. But how could he? It was once. A chance meeting under a lemon tree and then she was gone.

He remembered days blurring into weeks. His credit was running out. He needed to find the work he came here for, and yet he couldn't leave the hotel. The sun was always too bright, the days too hot, and all he could think about was finding *her* again. Seeing her one more time.

The nights were somehow less torturous. Sometimes he sat on the balcony, breathing the thin air. He had lost weight since that day, but didn't notice that his clothing was hanging loose, nor that his belt was tightened to the smallest notch.

Food came to his room sometimes. Rare steaks and a tonic vitamin supplement. A tangy liquid the colour of blood.

Sometimes he ate. Sometimes he didn't.

After a while the dreams became less frequent.

In them he felt her hair draping over his bare chest, her lips pressed to his throat. Her sex clasped around him.

After such dreams, his skin became tender and bruised, as though the wish he made had come true after all and she had been there for real: not just a delusion.

'I'm losing my mind,' he said. The thought amused him as he was speaking to no-one. That was when he realised it was true.

It's Novo Mars. The air. The people. The religion. It was

draining him of life.

'You need to eat more,' he remembered her telling him.

He was dreaming, of course. Why else would this beauty be lying naked in *his* bed?

Dutifully he sat up and allowed himself to be spoon-fed. He took a mouthful of steak, chewed, swallowed. She offered the red drink. These days it tasted better, less metallic, more nourishing. Perhaps he needed it after all?

'Sleep Luke,' she said. 'You'll need your strength. I won't come back. Any more and I will kill you.'

He wakes alone in a stark white room. He is wired to a machine which beeps.

The door to the room opens.

'Hello Luke,' says the nurse. She has dark hair. Blue eyes. She isn't *her*.

'Where am I?' he says.

'You've been sick. Mars fever. It's rare these days, but you had a bad case of it.'

'Mars fever? No. There was a woman. Dark hair, eyes like night …'

'Better sleep. You'll feel better in a few days.'

He closes his eyes, but he hears the nurse as she talks, adding notes to his file: a flat screen on the wall above his bed fills with detail. Nobody types or writes anymore, they just talk.

'The patient has acute anaemia and the same delusion as previous sufferers of the disease. His mind has focused on a dark-haired woman. The *Siren of Novo Mars* strikes again. Treatment: intensive dietary supplements and possible synth transfusion. Treat patient as a drug addict. He will crave the attention of his imagined vampire.'

'I'm well, doctor,' Luke says. 'No more dreams. No more fever madness.'

'You understand that these delusions were all brought on by the fever?' the doctor says. He is typical in appearance. Fat. Fifties. Fatherly.

'Yes,' says Luke. 'I know that this wasn't real. This ... woman ... never existed.'

'You'll need to keep taking your medication for six months. Otherwise the virus can come back. You might not be so lucky next time. If that maid hadn't found you...'

'I know. I will take my medication,' Luke lied.

He has been in the hospital for more than a month and is now desperate to leave. He will say anything. The doctor knows this but cannot justify keeping him any longer; he can only hope that the Siren's hold has been broken.

Luke packs his bag, signs the release form, and the doctor wonders if he will survive on Novo Mars. Few like him do.

From behind the reception desk the dark-haired nurse watches him leave. She doesn't say goodbye.

'That's pretty,' says the nurse next to her. 'Your necklace. Is it a ruby?'

A different hotel. A new room. He remembers her scent: pheromones that promise heaven. Metallic. Dark.

He takes his pills. Sleeps. Tries to forget. But the Siren never leaves his thoughts. She will be with him always. Sometimes he still dreams that she visits him but the dreams are few and far between. He wonders where she is. Who her new lover might be.

When he goes out, those rare journeys between work and home, he looks for her. There are lemon trees near the hotel … Gnarled.

He will search until his mind is lost.

Lighting the Beacon

Freda Warrington

'The great upturned bowl of the Plains sky was drenched with the blood of sunset. The sun itself had fallen beyond the Edge of the World. Now, before the rising of the moon, only a single star gemmed the cloak of gathering twilight.'
— from The Storm Lord *by Tanith Lee.*

This was the first sentence, first paragraph, first novel by Tanith Lee that I ever read. Her words instantly captivated me. In fact as soon as I read them there in the bookshop, I just had to buy the book.

By the mid-1970s I was already writing fantasy, trying to emulate ground-breaking writers such as Michael Moorcock, Ray Bradbury, Ursula LeGuin, Joy Chant and others, but Tanith's prose was like poetry. As spellbinding as the *Rubaiyat of Omar Khayyam*, no less.

The world she created in *The Storm Lord* is moved, not by evil sorcerers or magic rings, but by human behaviour, by accidents of birth, human power struggles and failings. Here were attractive, flawed characters who did terrible things and suffered for their mistakes, and yet managed to remain fascinating to the reader. And accidents of birth, naturally, meant sex: lots of it. I'd rarely come across characters who had actual desires and relationships in fantasy fiction before. There was certainly very little of that in Tolkien! But Tanith's erotic scenes, even when they were disturbingly violent, didn't dwell on salacious detail. Her writing was – is – so good that she didn't need to.

Admittedly there were aspects to the narrative that troubled me, and still made me uncomfortable when I recently re-read the novel. Reluctant temple prostitutes. Acts of rape, even one committed by the hero Raldnor himself. A queen being raped and enjoying it. Women relentlessly labelled as whores by their brutish Vis overlords. It's gut-wrenching stuff, but I found it to reflect what was a disconcertingly normal mindset in the mid-1970s.

On rereading, a subtler and more subversive agenda emerges. Tanith gives us a powerful feminist subtext. For these brutal sexual degradations don't go unpunished: indeed, they have repercussions throughout the plot, building until the great, golden serpent-goddess Anackire herself rises up to overthrow Raldnor's enemies in a cataclysm of biblical proportions.

Yet Tanith does her world-building with a light touch. No maps, no lists of characters, no heavy back-story to wade through. Again, she didn't need all that baggage: she creates worlds with just a few words, a skill that many fantasy writers would be wise to learn.

Above all, I was captivated by her stunning way with words, the sheer beauty of her descriptions. Even after a gap of thirty years, I not only remembered scenes from The Storm Lord, but entire phrases. *'In her navel a drop of yellow resin spat.'* *'Outside the snow sugared the world with its levelling pallor.'* Too many to quote them all.

I'd been writing since childhood, and *A Blackbird in Silver* (which became my first published novel) was already in progress when I discovered her work. But when I was drawn into the breathtaking world of *The Storm Lord*, I saw how high Tanith had set the bar! This was the kind of writer I wanted to be, and I'm still trying.

In those pre-internet days, authors were like gods. I would never have dreamed of writing to one, let alone meeting them. When I did eventually meet Tanith, some ten years later at a convention, I could barely breathe. With her strikingly beautiful face and powerful presence, she was quite literally like a goddess. I was terrified of her! But I thought, 'Well, I'll go and say hello. The worst she can do is tell me to get lost.'

She didn't. On the contrary, she was warm, friendly, welcoming – in fact she could not have been nicer to a very new, anxious author. She took me to lunch, on more than one occasion. It wouldn't be an exaggeration to say that she swept me off my feet! What amazing times those were.

But that, as I learned, was Tanith to the core. She had a massive heart and took new writers under her wing, like a mother goddess, a benevolent mentor. And I'm so glad I had a chance to tell her how much she and her writing meant to me before she was taken from us too soon. I feel that, through her work and her powerful, charismatic presence, she will always be with us.

So, asked to write a story based on my favourite novel of hers, I could only choose *The Storm Lord*. But a story featuring the actual characters? I wasn't convinced I could do them justice. Instead a different idea drifted into my head... a kind of dystopia set in a world not entirely unlike our own, at some nebulous time in the recent past or future… and this story was the result.

Tanith was very much loved and always will be. Her work does far more than simply inspire people. Writing isn't always easy, yet she never stopped. And because she poured ideas and whole worlds onto paper, and because she still had so much to say, for her sake – however frustrating this writing business can be at times – for Tanith's sake I will do my best to carry my own small relay beacon onwards into the dark.

'They who endure more, are more; they who suffer most can accomplish most.'

– Tanith Lee.

Ruins and Bright Towers

Freda Warrington

The rain was endless. It poured between the tall buildings on either side of the street as if falling into a bronze canyon, eerily half-lit by orange streetlights, dirty and dark yet shining like oil. This was where Sylvie always saw the girl.

Sylvie had lived all her life on this road and she knew every building: the vast derelict factory along one side, the other side crammed with big old terraced houses: separate households no longer but accommodation for the transient inhabitants of student digs, flats, the children's care home. Further along stood a pub, a row of shops and the shabby old community centre.

A low-level industrial hum made the air throb. It seemed to tremble up from the ground and into Sylvie's bones. Metallic, disturbing, just loud enough to be unpleasant. The factory was long-closed so it did not come from there, unless ghost workers still operated machines behind the darkened windows. Power lines, maybe. No one ever mentioned the noise. People must be so used to it that they didn't hear it any more. The sound, like the rain, was never-ending.

Sylvie was just fifteen. The girl, nicknamed Red, was a year younger. They knew each other only slightly. Other kids came and went from the home at all hours – she often crossed the road to avoid their attention – but Red was always alone. She was short, skinny, usually dressed in shabby jeans and a t-shirt, or a baggy sweater when it was really cold.

Sylvie saw her now on the edge of the pavement, arms wrapped around herself, rain beading like dew on her sweater. Her face in profile looked about twelve, upturned nose, pouty lips, no smile. Dusky brown skin implied mixed parentage; her hair was dyed crimson, hanging in long thick dreadlocks that were just starting to lose their colour and show black roots.

Red looked up and down the street. Nothing to see but slanting sheets of rain, and Sylvie standing a hundred yards away at the bottom of the steps that led up to her dad's flat. Sylvie raised a hand to wave a cautious 'hi.' Red looked away

A car came. Red got into it and was gone.

'How long's it take to walk to the bloody shops and back?'

Sylvie let herself into the hall of the tiny top-floor flat and stood dripping onto the lino. Her father was there waiting, with that grinning, joking yet snide manner he had. He held a can of strong cider in one hand, a joint in the other.

She said nothing. What sort of mood was he in? If good, he would laugh a lot at nothing, as if tickled by some private comedy show in his head. Bad: there would be self-pity, followed by blame and yelling. Sometimes worse.

'You got my stuff, Syl?'

She handed him a six-pack of cider, went to put away

a pint of milk and some dented cans of beans in the tiny kitchen. How did the sink get so full of dirty dishes, when he hardly ate anything? Perhaps it was her own negligence. He would blame her, in any case. She stared indifferently at the mess.

'Why don't you put a damn coat on when you go out? Don't want my little girl getting cold. You going to mop up that puddle you've dripped on the floor?'

And he went back into the living room to watch football, or one of the noisy quiz shows he liked. A good mood, then. He'd forgotten that he'd sold her coat at the community centre sale two weeks ago – along with her only weatherproof boots, and some books she'd failed to hide from him – and kept the money instead of giving it to the organisers like he was supposed to.

Sylvie went into her bedroom and shut the door. She got a towel and began to squeeze the water out of her hair. Her hair, once brown, had turned pure white when she was nine. That was the year her mother had left home. She'd been taunted at school – both about the greying hair and the slut mother – but she rarely went to school these days, so it didn't matter.

She pushed off her trainers using her toes; her socks were wet underneath. She pulled them off too, but there were no clean dry ones so she sat barefoot, cross-legged on the mattress that was her bed.

The flat, although cramped, had an echoey feel. No carpets. No curtains in the front room, since her dad had accidentally set them alight a few years ago. Her room had ancient, thin curtains with cartoon characters on them: trains with grinning faces. The curtains didn't meet in the middle, so streetlight painted her room orange. Outside the rain roared and the industrial hum throbbed without respite, causing the building and even the bones of her skull to vibrate.

She picked up a paperback novel and began to read, holding it one-handed while working at her hair with the other hand.

The Storm Lord by Tanith Lee.

Actually it was half a book. She had no tape to stick the torn halves back together. The cover was bent and tattered, the pages crinkled, but she loved the cover: in lurid shades of green and orange and purple, the mysterious otherworldly figures of a warrior and a goddess rode an alien beast towards their destiny.

Sylvie read with slow, careful attention. She entirely forgot her father and the rainy wasteland outside. She lost herself in the world of the Vis, where Dortharians ruled savagely over the pale, passive Lowlanders of the Shadowless Plains. The Vis lords *'moved with a special, almost a specific arrogance which pronounced them alien to this landscape far more than did their black hair and black-bronze burnish of their skin ... for they were Dortharians, dragons, and they carried a High King in their midst.'*

A brutal world, but there was something in their brutality that spoke to her. The High King Rehdon, roused to unbearable lust by the mystical phases of the Red Moon, chose a Lowland woman, Ashne'e, to lie with him. There was no question of her saying no.

'She seemed carved from white crystal, translucent eyes, like discs of yellow amber, open wide on his, the tawny cloud of hair fixed as frozen vapour... "Tonight you lie with me," Rehdon said.'

Sylvie paused, biting the tip of her thumb. This portrayal of sex distressed her. The image of powerful men forcing themselves onto subjects who dared not refuse made her shudder with confusion. Disturbing, yet the scene filled her with nebulous excitement.

No wicked act in *The Storm Lord* went unpunished, however. *'Plains women, it was rumoured, knew strange arts. Knew, too, how to stare in at a soul stripped naked by the pleasure spasms of the flesh.'*

Rehdon the High King was not going to survive his night with Ashne'e. By morning he was dead, and the temple girl was carrying his son: Raldnor, the rejected child of mixed Vis and Lowland blood, who would grow to be a tall beautiful man with dark skin and pale hair, the fascinating tormented hero.

'Pleasure spasms of the flesh,' Sylvie read softly aloud to herself.

Her dad's fist banged on the door, making her jump.

'Oy, princess! You ever going to make supper? There's fucking beans but no fucking bread!'

She jumped to her feet as he barged into the room. The one time she'd tried to put a bolt on her side, he'd smashed it off with a hammer, then swung a hammer-blow at her head that broke her left middle finger as she put up her hand to protect herself. He hadn't taken her to hospital, so the finger had set crooked. The woodwork around the door was still splintered. It would never be mended.

'I had enough to buy bread or cider, not both,' she said. Her voice was flat and quiet. She dropped her head to one side, letting the straggly white hair cover her face.

Bad mood now. He started moaning on about her utter uselessness while she moved mechanically to find a last, ice-crusted pizza in the freezer, to heat it, cut it in half and arrange it on two plates with warmed-up beans.

They sat side by side on the sofa to eat, telly blaring.

Father still smoking his spliff. The smell made her feel sick. He pushed the beans around his plate with a look of disgust on his face. Then he said, 'This is shit,' and let the full plate slide off his knee to land in a splattered mess on the floor.

Sylvie pushed a chair against the inside of the door. She settled down on her mattress with her book and a can of his cider: she'd left him snoring. With luck he wouldn't wake until morning. She had left her own full plate on a side-table, just in case, because if he decided he was hungry after all and there was nothing left, she would bear the consequences.

Most likely the congealed food would still be there tomorrow.

He never actually meant to hurt her when he threw things or lashed out, but the rooms were small and she wasn't always quick enough to evade him. Then he'd squash her against his thin chest and soft beer belly, overcome with emotion, his tears dripping into her hair, protesting that he was, '*Sorry, sorry, sorry, Syl, my poor little girl.*'

One thing he didn't do was interfere with her body. She'd heard about that from the care home girls. Dads, step-dads, uncles, cousins, even teachers: pawing, sticking their fingers where their fingers had no right to be, doing god knows what else, as if their flesh-and-blood children were blow-up dolls. She'd heard the kids speak casually about this horror as if it was only to be expected – as impassive as the Lowland women in the story.

'*The Lowland girl lay like a corpse beneath him, while her hair seemed to set the pillow alight.*'

At least her dad didn't do that to her. She considered

herself lucky.

He didn't do much of anything, except drink.

Sylvie read for most of the night. She recoiled at the scene where Raldnor – he was meant to be the hero, after all, yet he... he was in love with the white-haired Lowland girl, Anici – '*She was all whiteness ... and all of her framed by hair like blown and nacreous tinsel.*' – yet despite Anici's innocence and fear, the Red Moon possessed him and he raped her.

Sylvie put down the book and hugged her knees. Her eyes were sightless. Something formless moved inside her... fear and fascination. Her head whirled with vivid images.

The young, reluctant, shrinking girl, overpowered by a man who was supposed to love her... Raldnor's agonising regret, which came too late. Then his callous visit to a prostitute, supposedly to spare Anici from his lust ... were men really like this in real life, even the good ones?

Sylvie found her place, bookmarked with an old scrap of paper that bore her mother's handwriting. The story was horrifying yet she could not stop turning the pages.

And then, Anici's encounter with the new Storm Lord – Raldnor's half-brother, the dark and twisted Amrek – who sent his men to kidnap her for his pleasure. The moment the Storm Lord touched Anici, she died of sheer terror.

'*Under the dull bleeding of the incense braziers, she lay like a white inverted shadow, stretching out from his blackness on the floor. He bent over her and found that she was dead.*'

And Raldnor was not there to save her because he'd gone to visit a brothel.

He was tormented with guilt forever afterwards. And

so he should be, Sylvie thought. Yet she still felt for him in his pain. And for Anici too, the wide-eyed victim of these mighty, terrible men.

It was all wrong. But that was the power of the story. All the horror and injustice and catastrophic mistakes – they were what made her care, made her read compulsively until she finally fell asleep near dawn.

She'd only got the book because of Red. The sale in the community centre had been a fund-raiser for the children's home. Some of the kids were there helping out, and Red had been standing behind a table piled with old paperback books.

Sylvie and her dad had no money to spend. They were there to be nosy, see what they could steal, her dad also to commit fraud for beer money. As she approached the book table, she saw Red take a paperback off the pile and slip it into a carrier bag. But there was another care home kid nearby, a skinny older boy, and he saw what Red had done. He grabbed the book out of her bag and held it in the air, taunting her. Angry, she jumped up to take it back, but he was too tall. He ripped the book in half and flung it down. Both halves fell at Sylvie's feet.

No one said anything. The boy sauntered away. Red's face was expressionless. Sylvie picked up both halves of the book and took them home.

Nine o'clock in the morning, and Red was on the street near the children's home. She wasn't on her way to school, though. She was blatantly just arriving back from somewhere. A few yards away Sylvie saw the blue car, and four men standing around it, Red talking to them.

One of the men was white; gaunt, stubbly and cold-eyed. Two were dark-skinned, Asian-looking. The fourth

214

she couldn't tell; he had his back to her, a baseball cap hiding his hair, but he looked short, stocky and middle-aged. The two dark men held her attention. Young and confident, with broad smiles, thick black hair and shining eyes.

They made her think of the Vis, the Dortharians in the story. Dragon Lords, like Raldnor. Frightening yet attractive, full of raw power like panthers. One of them touched Red on the shoulder as she walked away, and Sylvie felt a tiny pang of jealousy.

'What you staring at?' Red said, giving Sylvie a quick hard glance as she passed.

'Who are those men?'

The car pulled away. The street was empty. Nothing moved but the drizzle, and half a dozen pigeons taking sudden flight from the factory roof opposite. Sylvie felt she and Red were the only two people left alive in the world.

'No one. Just some friends.'

She sniffed. She looked grey with tiredness, and slurred her words. Her eyes were as red as her hair.

'Are you supposed to be out with them?'

'What are you, my care worker?' A small sneer. 'Mind your own fucking business, yeah?'

'Okay. Sorry.'

'What d'you want, anyway?'

'To give you this.' Sylvie held out the half-book, the front section with the lurid orange and green cover. 'You wanted to read it, didn't you? I saw you take it in the community centre, before that idiot grabbed it off you. I've got the other half. I'll give it you as soon as I've finished.'

Red stared at the cover, as if trying to remember why

it was important. She said softly, 'Is it any good?'

'Yes, brilliant.'

'Go on, then.' She took the gift and made for the concrete steps up to the front door. Sylvie looked longingly after her: she didn't want to go back to her father, but she had nowhere else to go. She called after the retreating back, cloaked by long scarlet dreadlocks,

'Are you all right?'

'Yeah, fine. Thanks for the book.'

Her mother's drinking was the reason her parents had split up: ironic, considering that her dad drank even more. There had been screaming arguments, broken furniture, accusations about other men. One day, just after Sylvie's ninth birthday, she came home from school and her mother wasn't there anymore.

Sylvie hadn't seen her since.

As a child, she must have been upset and cried, but she didn't remember that. All she remembered was a kind of numbness gathering around her until she didn't feel anything, except the emotions she drew second-hand from characters in books.

'Outside the snow sugared the world with its levelling pallor.'

She liked that line. That was how she felt. Everything quite cold, controlled and still inside her. Level.

She was onto the second part of the torn-in-half book now and there was a new character: Astaris, a red-haired Vis woman, a princess. 'Pricelessly rare,' one of the characters told Raldnor, who by a strange chain of events would become a guard in the service of his enemy, the High King Amrek. 'A mane the colour of rubies.'

Pricelessly rare – as if Astaris had value only as an

exquisite work of art, not as a human being.

Astaris was to marry Amrek. She was self-contained and completely enigmatic – until she and Raldnor set eyes upon each other. No, not the first time they saw each other... but the first time they were accidentally alone together. But even before they met, they touched each other's minds and they both *knew*.

'Her hair was the precise colour of blood... and she was in his skull like flame and he in hers... The longing came swift and devouring and fed on itself in each of them.'

Sylvie wondered how that would feel... to meet your soulmate and simply *know* there could be no one else in all the world. But in the world of the Vis, you did not fall in love with the High King's future bride without dire consequences.

Betrayed, Raldnor and Astaris had to flee for their lives, each thinking the other dead.

'She lived within herself, and no part of her reached out to commune with others...'

I'm kind of like that, thought Sylvie. So is Red, I think.

She read on in a feverish rush, wanting the story to go on forever, yet wanting to finish so that her friend could read it too and then they would have something to talk about. Something magical.

'Is Red your real name?'

'It is now.'

She and Red walked through the rainy streets together, aimless, but farther afield than Sylvie usually went on her own. The city thrummed and shook, but its relentless pulse seemed muted. 'You got any friends at the home? How long have you lived there?'

'You ask a lot of questions, don't you? I've been there

about a hundred years and they all hate me, but I don't care anymore. Okay?'

'You're not the only one who gets bullied, you know,' said Sylvie. 'I'm dead scared of those kids, too. And I got hell at school. First because my mum walked out, then because my hair turned white – they'd yank strands of it right out of my head and call me 'grandma' – then because everyone knows my father's an alky, then because I liked schoolwork and I was good at reading, then because – I don't know. They didn't even need a reason. I know how you feel.'

'You don't know anything about me,' said Red.

Sylvie shrugged. 'I know you love books. And I know you've got no friends, same as me. But I like you, even though you're rude and miserable. I like you anyway.'

'Fuck off,' said Red.

Most of their conversations went like this. Fragments here and there, skipping between one thing and another. They were both finding their way.

Buildings towered around them, staring down with blank windows. Weeds struggled out of the tarmac. They walked down to the canal and along the towpath. Deserted red factories stood all along the far bank and some ancient narrow boats were moored there, bobbing against the slimy green brickwork. People lived in them.

Looking at the canal, Sylvie said, '*The sky had turned black, and spears of pallid light flickered beyond the river; rain began to fall in huge molten drops, and the river boiled.*'

'That's from *The Storm Lord*, right?'

'Sometimes when I see things, I think how Tanith Lee would describe them. Makes the world a bit more romantic and less sordid.'

Red grinned. Sylvie hardly ever saw her smile, so she was pleased.

'You know a lot of big words, don't you? Don't tell me how it finishes.'

'I wasn't going to.'

'By the way.' Red took a scrap of paper from her jeans pocket and pushed it into Sylvie's hand. 'You left your bookmark in it. There's an address on it, so I thought you might need it.'

'Thanks.'

Pause. 'Is it where your mum lives now?'

'No. I don't know where she lives. But she wrote the note, and she left hardly anything else behind, so that's why I kept it. Stupid, really.'

'At least you know who your parents are. That's more than I do.'

'Yeah, and I sometimes wish I didn't,' said Sylvie. 'Ever feel like you're stuck, like really trapped, and life will just go on and on and on exactly the same until you drop dead?'

'I just feel like I wish it would stop fucking raining.'

'I understand why my dad drinks. I steal his cider sometimes. It gives me a bad head, but I could get used to it. You got any guilty secrets?'

'Like what?'

'Those men.'

She thought Red was going to clam up again. She was quiet for a while as they walked. Plastic bags drifted across the canal, carried by the wet breeze. Sylvie saw a narrow road leading up between the factories and a street name, *Wharfside Lane*, but it might as well have been another country. Then Red looked at Sylvie with a strange glow in her eyes. 'They're all right. They give me stuff. Presents, sometimes. All the drink you want, and other stuff that makes you feel amazing, like you're flying.'

'But what do they want in return?' No answer. 'Do you really think you ought to...?'

'What? Like you said, there's nothing else to do.'

'That's why I read stories. I can go into another world...' She decided to change tack. 'You enjoying the book?' Red nodded. 'What do you like best about it?'

'All the sex,' Red answered with a smirk.

Sylvie rolled her eyes. 'What else?'

'I like Astaris. I like the way she's so cool and just doesn't mind about anything. When Amrek the Storm Lord gets mad because she takes no notice of him, he tells her that even her beauty will get boring and then he'll kill her. And all she does is smile. Yes, I like that.'

'*She lived within herself, and no part of her reached out to commune with others,*' Sylvie quoted and Red laughed, understanding.

Sylvie felt a little thrill of conspiracy.

'You *are* Astaris,' she said. 'The dark skin, the blood-red hair. You're her.' She pulled at her own damp, pale hair with a colourless hand. 'And me, I must be Anici.'

'So Raldnor should be along to rescue us any day, right?'

'Anici bent over him and touched his shoulder. He got up in the darkness, and she stood waiting, the wind washing through her silver hair. The white moon shone behind her; he saw the shadow of her small bones beneath her skin. As he approached her, she raised her arms, and long cracks appeared in her body, like ink lines on alabaster. Then she crumbled all at once into gilded ashes, and the ashes blew away across the moon, leaving

only darkness to wake him.'

'Oy, princess!' Her father was yelling at the door. 'Go down the shop for me cider, will you?'

Sylvie started up on her mattress in panic. She'd been asleep, dreaming. Red had the second portion of the book now so she found herself dreaming about the characters instead; dead Anici haunting Raldnor, about the enigmatic Astaris with her blood-red hair, about Amrek's soldiers slaughtering pale Lowlanders there in the street outside her window, the gutters running with blood and rain.

'Dad, I can't. They know I'm not eighteen, they won't serve me anymore!'

'Don't talk crap, Syl, they don't care who they serve. Get us a half-bottle of the cheap vodka while you're at it.'

'It's dark. It's raining.'

She sat huddled, waiting for him to burst in and yell at her.

'What're you *doing* in there?' he said through the door. 'You got a boy in there, you little slut?' Then he gave a sort of exasperated guffaw and shuffled away. She waited a few moments, clenching her teeth in anger. Eventually she got up, as resigned and passive as Anici herself, and went to do his bidding.

She and Red spent the whole afternoon together next day. Her father was still sleeping off the previous night; no adult seemed to care that they wandered the streets and stole chocolate from the newsagent and walked along the canal where it wasn't safe and never went to school. No one cares that we exist, Sylvie thought, but maybe we can look out for each other.

She was impatient for Red to finish *The Storm Lord.* As

it was, they talked idly about which part she'd reached, and why each character did what he or she did.

Mad, tormented Amrek had set about slaughtering every single Lowlander in the world out of fear and rage. A Lowlander – Ashne'e – had killed his father, he believed. Another Lowlander – Raldnor – had stolen Astaris. Now in savage vengeance he lashed out, intending genocide on their whole race.

'The storm gods of Dorthar that directed Amrek in his holy war – they would no longer brook the scum of the snake goddess.'

And Raldnor – now possessed by that very goddess – had to stop him by gathering an army of his own, but it was a long, terrible struggle and anyway, what was it all for when he believed Astaris to be dead?

But Anackire, the snake-goddess – She and Red agreed that was their favourite part, the gigantic statue hidden in a long-forgotten temple underground.

'And then the soaring whiteness of the giantess with her whirling golden tail. Anackire, the Lady of Snakes... She towered. She soared. Her flesh was a white mountain, her snake's tail a river of fire in spate.'

Their talk stopped. All thoughts of the book vanished.

The blue car was there again, a few yards along from the kids' home, the same four men leaning against the bodywork with arms folded. Red tensed like a bird about to take flight. Sylvie couldn't tell if she was spellbound by fear or excitement. Maybe both.

At once all Red's attention was fixed on them, as if her companion had ceased to exist.

Sylvie resented this. Of course the men were infinitely more exciting than a dull, bookish girlfriend, but she hated them for that. She wanted to tell Red to ignore them, tell them to fuck right off with their sly smiles and lazy, knowing eyes. If she and Red were Anici and Astaris, the men were Dortharians: dark and powerful and able to take whatever they wanted. A touch from them and you would die of fear.

Yet she tingled with curiosity. Truth was, she was jealous of Red with her knowing smiles and her secret world. She wanted to taste this forbidden... whatever it was. The closest she'd ever come to 'partying' was a stolen can of strong white cider in her bedroom. And Red was the only friend she'd ever had, because people around here were so closed-in and hostile, too busy armouring themselves from the hostility of everyone else in the world to risk a kind word.

Ignoring the pallid man and the creepy middle-aged one, Sylvie could only look at the two panthers. She thought about Dortharian dragon lords with their dangerous, erotic beauty. She remembered the glow in Red's eyes as she said, *'They give me stuff. Presents, sometimes. All the drink you want, and other stuff that makes you feel amazing, like you're flying.'*

Helpless, she watched Red walk to the men and give herself into their hands. Then one of them, all shadowy languorous beauty, looked at her and called out, 'Hey, what's your name?'

'Sylvie.'

'You want to come and party with your friend, Sylvie?'

'You disgusting little slut.'

Daylight blinded her. Her father's face was an inch from hers, red with fury, his sour breath smothering her. She rolled away, retching. Her head throbbed in time to the metallic pulse of the city, steel hammers beating her brain. The previous night – a blank. She didn't even remember how she'd got home. Sore everywhere.

And her father had a fistful of ten-pound notes, and was shaking them in her face.

'Yer gone all night. Roll back in at eight, stoned out of yer head, reeking of god-knows-what, and *this* in your pocket. I know where you've been! Whoring, just like your mother! Exactly like your fucking mother. Apple doesn't fall far, does it?'

He took the money and left, slamming the door.

Sylvie lay still for a long time, thinking of nothing. She only moved when her bladder was bursting and her mouth so dry she couldn't swallow. By then her dad had gone out. Pub. Bookies. Shops, for more booze. Her night of shame was a bonanza for him.

There was no hot water. Once she'd washed in cold and put on her other pair of jeans and a fresh sweatshirt, she let herself out and walked down the street to the kid's home.

She stood looking up at the windows. Nothing stirred inside. The rain grew heavier and she began to shiver.

'Red?' she called. No answer. She didn't know which room her friend slept in, and she daren't shout too loud in case some of the bigger boys heard.

The hell she daren't. She marched up the steps and pounded on the front door, but no one came, not even an adult. Eventually she retreated and walked away, feeling deflated and stupid.

There was a woman on the other side of the road, staring at her. A stranger with long thick hair, very pale: blond or even pure white. A floating dress with handkerchief points, the colour of mist, like white muslin in shadow, as if the garment were partly made of rain and moving gently on a breeze. An apparition, not of this world. Eyes rimmed with black, like an Egyptian goddess. Such intense eyes. Terrifying, challenging, chiding, full of fierce warmth. Staring, staring, staring into her.

White pigeons rose up from the pavement in a whirring flock. They spiralled around the woman in a flurry of wings and when they vanished, so had she.

Sylvie stood looking down at her father. He lay flat-out on the sofa, one hand trailing on the filthy floor, mouth open, drooling. There was a nearly-empty bottle of whisky lying among the cigarette ends, roaches and cider cans. The front room was a stifling, fetid cave.

His eyes were open a slit, gleaming. He seemed to be looking at her, but his breathing was off. He wasn't so much snoring as groaning. *Ahhhhh* ... he groaned, as if to say, *help me*.

Was he asleep or in some kind of coma? His skin looked yellow and, despite being so thin, his belly was grossly swollen. Perhaps he'd had a fit. Perhaps he was dying.

'I'm sorry, Dad,' she said softly, without emotion. 'I can't look after you anymore.'

No response.

'Dad, I'm leaving now.'

The street was a red brick chasm, the road surface iron-grey and boiling with rain, the sky swollen with a sickly orange glow. She felt a sharp chill in the air. On a corner where a side-road joined the main street, a gang of boys from the care home stood around, aimless and menacing.

They were sniggering at something on a smart phone, but as she passed they all looked up and stared.

'Oy, blondie!' one of them yelled at her. It was the scrawny boy who'd taken the book from Red and torn it in half. 'Whitey! Hey, granny! Grandma, where's your walking stick?'

Usually she scurried past them as fast as she could, hiding her face behind a veil of white hair. Today, though, she stopped, turned, marched across the road.

'Give me your phone,' she said.

The scrawny boy gave a horrible mocking laugh. 'You what?'

She smelled the smoke and sweat that clung to them. Sensed them clustering around their prey, excited.

But she wasn't scared. How did she look to them? She felt that she suddenly wore the face of Anackire, savage and terrifying with fire for eyes and writhing snakes for hair. She showed her teeth and their confidence wavered.

'I said, *give me the fucking phone.*'

The blue car was already there. Red was on her way towards it, arms folded, head bowed, faded-scarlet hair draping her khaki sweatshirt.

'*The rain beat down. Her fabulous hair seemed full of fires.*'

Sylvie remembered almost nothing of the previous night, except little flashes that kept stabbing like pins through her eyes. The men no longer looked enticing or even interesting to her. The sight of them made her nearly sick.

And yet Red was going to them again, as passive and insouciant as Astaris. Sylvie felt dismayed and helpless, but most of all she was furious.

'Red,' she called, running to catch her up. 'Red, don't

227

go with them. Please.'

Red glared at her with hard eyes. 'What's your problem? You had fun, didn't you?'

Sylvie shook her head. 'Maybe the first half-hour. But the stuff they made us do... That wasn't fun.'

'You get used to it. It's not that bad.'

'Yes, it is!'

'Thing is, you can't start and then stop,' Red answered in a harsh whisper. She held up a clenched fist. 'They get you like *this*. You're a coward. If you can't take it, go back to your dad.'

The men were all leaning on the car, waiting. Smiling their contemptuous, predatory smiles.

Red started towards them again. Sylvie grabbed her wrist, hard.

'I've left my dad.'

'So?'

She showed Red the stolen phone. 'He's sick. I've called an ambulance. But I've got to get away from here, and so have you. If you don't come with me *now*, I'll call the police.'

Red started breathing very fast, her eyes widening.

'You call the police, those guys will kill us.'

Sylvie stared her down and hissed, '*I. Don't. Care.*'

'Hey,' called one of the men. 'You little sluts coming with us, or what?'

'Raldnor isn't on his way to save us. We have to save ourselves.' Sylvie dug her nails in and jerked Red's arm as hard as she could. '*Run*,' she snarled.

They ran.

Sidestreets, footpaths, the unlit spaces beneath a railway bridge – the labyrinth swallowed them. Wasteland and weeds streaked past in a blur, gleaming dully from the strange orange glow of the sky. The rain was bitterly cold. It stung like needles. Sylvie's wet hair whipped around her face, but she hardly noticed the discomfort of her sore lungs or the penetrating cold. She ran and ran with a kind of insane glee. Red laughed too, in between gasps, as if they were fleeing the scene of some outrageous prank.

The men intercepted them on the canal towpath.

The car was already there – they must have squeezed it down some alleyway – headlights shining on the muddy path. The two white guys were by the car on their right, the two dark ones ten yards away on their left, all four grinning like jackals. Sylvie and Red were trapped in between.

In front of them the canal lay like a slow black snake.

She thought of Raldnor plunging into the river Okris, trying to escape Amrek's soldiers after he and Astaris had been found out. *'Sluggish and very cold beneath... When he lifted his head for air, he rose against a stone wall, viscous with muddy weeds...'*

Sylvie seized Red's arm. Together they rushed forward and leapt.

The water was a black, icy shock. She floundered. Dark turbid water as thick as oil, full of floating detritus: plastic bags and bottles and stuff better not to know what it was.

'I can't sw–'

Red was sinking, panicking, thrashing to keep her face in the air. Sylvie grabbed the collar of her sweatshirt, held her head clear, and dragged her through the sewer murk of the canal. Water kept splashing into her face. Floating objects collided with her as she swam, awkward and one-handed, fighting to keep Red's face clear of the surface.

On the other side she reached a moored narrow boat, got hold of a rope that was trailing in the water, and helped Red to scramble onto the back of the vessel. It rocked under their slight weight as they found their balance. From there, they pulled themselves up three feet of slimy brick wall and onto firm ground. They paused, shivering, sobbing, coughing.

The men stood on the far bank, silhouetted against the car headlights. Just standing there, like four stick men in a cartoon, rigid with frustrated anger.

One of them called out, 'We'll hunt you down, you little bitches.'

Red cackled. Sylvie had never heard her laugh so loud before, with such abandon. Then she yelled at the top of her voice.

'Fuck off!'

And Sylvie gave them the finger; the crooked middle finger that had healed wrong after her father broke it.

Lights came on inside the narrow boat. By the time the grumbling occupant emerged, the men had slouched back to their car and dissolved into the gloom, while Sylvie and Red were a hundred yards clear, running hand in hand along the narrow Wharfside Lane.

Above them, the rain turned into snow and came down in white swirls.

'I've got summat to tell you,' said Red. They were walking fast now, out of breath. Soaked, frozen, but too full of adrenaline to feel the cold. The world was turning soft and white around them. Snow muffled the harsh pulse of the city until she couldn't hear it anymore; the silence was unnerving.

'Yeah?'

'I'm a girl.'

'Duh.' Sylvie laughed. 'Me too. So what?'

'Well, cos I was born a boy.'

'Oh,' said Sylvie. The universe shifted. 'Oh, right.'

'Is that a problem?' Red's voice had a flat, belligerent edge.

'That's why you got bullied in the home?'

'Yeah.' Red sniffed. 'Pretty much. I was born the wrong sex. They said I was a boy but I always knew I was a girl. You want to see my dick and have a good laugh, like they did?'

'Don't be daft.' Pause. 'I'm sorry that happened to you.'

'I don't want sympathy. Like you said – if it wasn't that, would've been something else. We were all as bad as each other in different ways. Just wanted you to know.'

'Thanks.' They went on in silence. Sylvie took Red's hand. 'I don't mind. We're still who we are. You're Astaris, I'm Anici.'

'You're crazy,' said Red.

'There was a light, indeterminate, white moth snow blowing on the wind, melting colourlessly on the pavements of the city...' Sylvie remembered descriptions of snow from the story. *'Snow flamed on the wind. The wind was on fire with snow. When the snow stopped, the Plains lay in unbroken whiteness under an exhausted purple sky.'* That was exactly how the city seemed to her now. *'Over the city a snow moon burned like a lamp of blazing ice.'*

There was no moon, only lights shining from the windows of a house, and a soft lamp over its closed front door. Everything was covered with feathery, yellow-tinted whiteness.

They stood opposite the house, a high narrow Victorian villa with steps up to the entrance. *67, Wharfside Lane*.

That was the address her mother had scribbled on the scrap of paper. Sylvie had always known what it meant, even though, at the age of nine, she hadn't properly understood.

She understood well enough now. Knew, too, that her otherwise useless mother had left her this tiny lifeline on purpose. Just in case.

Light poured out of the windows but didn't reach the shadows where they stood on the opposite side of the road. Red, until now brisk and defiant, shrank into herself with nerves.

'Are you sure? There's no sign on the door.'

'Of course there isn't. People who've run away from being abused and beaten up don't want their boyfriends or whoever to *find* them. They're not going to put a sign on the door saying, "Women's Refuge, find your terrified wife here!" are they?'

In a small voice Red asked, 'Did your mum come here?'

'No idea. She just left me the address.'

'What are we going to say to them?'

Sylvie thought about *The Storm Lord*: the part where the passive Lowland slave girls rose up and slaughtered their Vis overlords. *'Their hair striped with hot blood, killing and killing, without thought or hesitation, like machines with eyes of blanched steel.'*

Out loud she said, 'Did you finish the book?'

'No. It's back at the home. You'll have to tell me how it ended.'

'If you don't mind spoilers.'

'I don't care. Tell me.'

There isn't time, Sylvie thought. And it was so brutal all the way through. Amrek was evil, but Raldnor was nearly as bad. His own armies brought as much violence and death, until he woke the goddess herself and she destroyed Dorthar with a massive earthquake. Anackire, the great goddess with her golden snake-tail, rising up out of her hidden temple to tower above Dorthar as the city fell.

'*Now the foaming water had lifted her a little and was thrusting her up against the roof of the cave. Her golden head grazed the granite above... Now the land slid and fell away. Out of the chasm emerged the massive milk-white torso with its burning eyes and hair... She crested the hills and rose incredibly into the pitch-black sky, a towering moon of ice and flame... Anackire soared and blazed, crushing them with the eight maledictions of her serpent arms. They had seen nemesis. Their world was ended. The goddess shone like a meteor in the black air, then sank, as the wave relinquished her, into the torn mirror of the lake.*'

Anackire had taken her revenge. Then the mad possession left Raldnor and he became human again...

Sylvie saw a remembered glimpse of the woman with the floating ghost-grey dress and intense kohl-rimmed eyes, the white pigeons fluttering around her. *You know what you have to do*, the eyes told her.

'The birds are always an omen,' said Sylvie.

'What?'

'There's too much. I'll just tell you the important bit.' Sylvie's teeth chattered with cold as she spoke.

'Raldnor kills Amrek and becomes the Storm Lord?'

'Too obvious. First he had to go and rescue Astaris.'

'I'm frozen,' said Red. 'You gonna stand here all night?'

'No,' said Sylvie, looking at the brightly-lit house. The door was locked – of course – but light spilled out all around its edges. 'There'll be people exactly like us in there. When we go in, I want to tell them what I'm telling you. I never expected the story to have a happy ending, but it did. When Raldnor found Astaris, he didn't care about becoming the Storm Lord. All they cared about was each other, so they ran away together and disappeared.'

'They did?' Red looked sideways at her from under lowered eyelids.

'Love meant more than power. Come on.'

Sylvie knew she would be too nervous to say a word when the door opened. But she imagined opening her arms to the spiralling snow and sharing her revelation with anyone who would listen.

Astaris and Raldnor escaped. We escaped.

So can you.

Sea and Blood and Night

Liz Williams

I have been reading Tanith Lee's work for years, from when I was a young reader: my mother got her books in paperback, and from the library. I remember seeing her for the first time at the Worldcon in the late 1980s in Brighton: I passed a very glamorous woman who looked like a rock star, saw her name badge and realised who she was. But I was too shy to say anything (same, IIRC, with Roger Zelazny).

Years later, after I had published my first novel, I got a phone call. 'Hello,' said a voice. 'I'm terribly sorry to ring you out of the blue. This is Tanith Lee. Your editor sent me your novel for a blurb and I don't usually do that, but I loved it ** and I wanted to talk to you about it. Can I take you out to dinner?'

I rarely squeak, let alone be struck dumb, but when my voice finally emerged, it can only be described as squeaky. 'Yes!' I said, in a high mouse-like falsetto. She must have thought I was nuts. Anyway, we went out to dinner, and we got on (6555ft --*) very well: it was the start of a long friendship, between Tanith, John, myself and my late partner Charles, and later, with Trevor.

Deirdre Counihan and her sister Liz, plus many other people, will remember afternoons and evenings in Brighton and Hastings, although I'm not sure that 'remember' is the right word in some of our cases due to the sheer amount of alcohol consumed. One of her favourites was the Bath Arms: if anyone called, she could say with perfect truth that she'd been in the Bath.

(* this bit was added by Cat on Keyboard. I'm leaving it in. Rosie may know something I don't. It would not surprise me if she and Tanith are in touch.)

(**I was not the only young writer to whom she was so generous: I think Jacqueline Carey was another at that time, and many more.)

I do, however, recall one evening in an Indian restaurant in the Lanes: we'd collected a number of people on the way, including Charles' friend Bill, who was a joiner and who had zero interest in science fiction or literature. Tanith sat next to him, at the other end of the table, and in a lull I heard her say, in those dramatic tones, 'Well, I think you're absolutely right. The referee was QUITE WRONG and I don't know what he was thinking.' She was very indignant. They were talking about Manchester United.

When we left Bill said 'WHO was that fascinating woman?'

When Charles died, Tanith volunteered to be the first to speak at his funeral. She gave an inspirational address, and broke the ice for many people to follow. With my mother Veronica and other friends, she came out to dinner with us on that difficult evening, forming a lasting connection between Veronica, a great admirer of her writing, and herself.

In the years that followed, we shared a book launch in Brighton, with friend and colleague Cherith Baldry (I think that was the one to which Harry Harrison turned up, having persuaded Chris Priest to spring him from the local hospital where he was recovering from a stroke: 'Godammit, Chris, I've gotta get out of here. Isn't there a party or something we can go to?' There was.) She came to my launch in London, organised by Ian Whates: it was such a pleasure to see her there. I think we talked about cats. As usual.

Today, it was – even under the circumstances – heartening to read her great friend Storm Constantine's recollections of her. Storm is one of our Generals, whose contribution to genre in this country deserves much more notice, and she has indeed been constant, along with editors like Ian Whates, Vera Nazarian and Craig Gidney, in keeping Tanith's flame alive. No-one knows better than the women SF and Fantasy writers of this country, and others, how hard it is to make a living in this industry – any sort of living. JK Rowling (good on her) is an exception. The neglect of Tanith's work – and it's down to the accounts and marketing departments of big publishers, not dedicated old school editors like Peter Lavery, whom we shared for a number of years – has been a continual source of baffled outrage to Tanith's colleagues. She was – is – one of the most genuinely original writers I've ever known. I don't know through what lens she saw the world, but they only made one such lens: curiously and unfamiliarly coloured, flavoured with the sea and blood and night. I do not think that the word 'genius' is misplaced. According to Storm, Tanith was working on edits last week. Dying's no excuse.

She is free now, to explore imagination's realms. She leaves her highly talented husband John Kaiine, to whom our support and love now, as ever, go, and of course, her many friends. A light has not gone out: it is elsewhere. It is up to us to find it. Thanks in part to her, we are not moths. We are the flame.

Tanith Lee & John Kaiine at Their Wedding

Waterwitch

Liz Williams

I had gone down to fetch more coal for the light when I first saw the ghost. This place is like an iceberg, and often as cold. The striped finger of the lighthouse rears up from the cliff, dizzying over the green churn of the sea, but few people know how far it reaches beyond and underground, as though its stocky weight is balanced by what lies below. Stairs, and a huge cellar, in which the coal is kept, and which leads into the island caves. Now – mid November and with the light dying fast – I did not have a great deal of coal left. I was eking it out, hoping the light would not grow much dimmer, hoping the boat would come from the tip of the land. But it was winter, we'd had storms, and the boat was late.

That evening, when there was still a strip of yellow light over the sea, I went down with a basket, to bring more coal back up. I filled the basket, carried it up to the entrance, then wrestled the door of the lighthouse open. I'd been confined for three days; I needed fresh air. And it was certainly fresh enough: the wind slapped me in the face like an angry lover and the air stank of seaweed and salt. However, the rain was dying from a wet lash to a steady downpour; in my waterproofs, it would take a while to bother me and I stood on the lighthouse step and gazed out to sea.

We are far in the northern seas, and land beyond the island is not visible. Only on very clear days, which are uncommon enough, do I sometimes think I see a pale blue shadow on the horizon's edge, which might be the Scottish coast. But maybe it's just my imagination. If you spend a long time on your own, or in a very small community, the world starts breaking down around you: you fancy that you see things that really are not there. Eventually you stop being able to tell the difference and that's when they usually send a boat, with a kind inspector on it, who brings you back to shore and smiles gently at you when you protest. Sometimes you don't protest much, at that. And you're generally all right after a week or so, speaking to other people, like nurses, and looking at things that aren't all ocean or spray, or the inside of the light. This is why I was currently alone here; the coal boat would bring not only fuel, but replacements for my fellow lighthouse keepers. Of those, one was now on emergency leave on shore; the other had been sent back, too, but with a broken ankle after a fall down those treacherous stairs. So I was the only man to tend the light now, and this would not do for long.

Yet it was not as though I did not have visitors. One of them was waiting for me, perched on a lip of rock in the rain. A stormy petrel, one of Mother Carey's chickens, as they are called in the north; they are said to hide in the lee of ships during gales. They are also said to be the spirits of sea captains who have abandoned their crew, and in some parts of the islands they are known as waterwitches. I believed none of their strange reputation,

244

but welcomed them as frequent visitors to the lighthouse, along with the gannets and gulls and all the other seabirds. This one was typical: a small bird, black with a stripe of white, almost invisible against the rock. It was bedraggled, its feathers ruffled. As I drew near, it whirled upwards, mewing like a cat, and was gone into the wind. I got the impression that it had been snatched up against its will, rather than flown.

Thinking about the bird, I made my way down the cliff path. It was good to get out of the confines of the lighthouse; I looked back, once, to see its reassuring bulk rising above me. But what I then saw, down on the rocks of the shore, slippery with bladder wrack, was a woman. She was sitting on a ledge of rock; her feet, which were bare, dangling over the waves. She wore a black dress that was a little too short. Her hair was white and it streamed out in the sea wind.

I could not believe my eyes. No-one else lived here – there was nowhere other than the lighthouse *to* live. I wondered for a mad moment if she had been deliberately marooned – but who would go to the trouble of abandoning an old lady on a desolate rock? Then, as if she had heard me, she looked up and I saw that she was not so old after all: her face was young. I only got a glimpse, but it was a pale face, and so were her eyes. A great wave of spray broke over her. I shouted, but she was gone. The sea had taken her, or she had been a ghost. There was no sign of a body floating in the frothing waves. I made my way down as best I could, heart thumping, but the ragged shore was empty. I searched until the light had truly died. By the time I stumbled back up the cliff path, I had convinced myself, almost, that I had imagined her.

That night, the storm hit with renewed force. I kept checking the light, but it was burning steadily enough. The diamond paned windows rattled with the force of the wind. We were safe enough but I still felt buffeted. It was not until morning that I managed to snatch some sleep, and then I dreamed of the woman. She was standing on the shore, gazing out to sea. This time, I walked easily over the rocks towards her and bade her hello.

'Don't interrupt,' she said, without glancing round. 'Can't you see I'm busy?'

'What are you doing?'

'Is it not obvious?'

'Not to me,' I said humbly.

'Oh,' she said, very offhand. 'I forgot – you probably can't see it. Your sort never can.'

And then I woke up. The dream baffled me, and it stayed with me over the course of the day. A couple of times, I even thought I saw her: a dress like a shadow flickering around a corner, but of course there was nothing there. When the coal boat arrived, I thought, it might be as well to send a letter to the inspector…

The storm was breaking up, doubtless in time for another one to arrive. I took advantage of the weather to roam my small domain, heading west to the spur of crag that jutted out into the ocean. I half expected to see the woman, but there was no-one there, not even a bird. The storm may have gone, but the sky was still dark, heavy with lowering cloud. I reminded myself that winter was well underway; we may yet get a few calm days before Christmas, but it wasn't likely. Standing on the spur, I looked out to sea. The far ocean was lost in a wall of mist, a streaming blankness which seemed, as fog often does, to blanket sound. Strange, given the recent gale. Shivering, I turned up my coat collar and headed back to the sanctuary of the lighthouse.

I would have welcomed the elusive company of the ghost, but she chose not to be visible, and I had not seen her when I opened the door for my brief walk. I made my meticulous notes on the weather – *storm over for the time being. Fog.* – and raided the dwindling bag of potatoes. The boat would bring more, but the boat was overdue. And so the day wore on, sinking almost imperceptibly into night, so dark it was.

Next day, I dreamed not of the woman, but of the petrel. In my dream, it came into the bedroom and drifted down onto the bed, light as a falling feather. I had not remembered leaving the lamp lit, but the room was suffused with an eerie glow. I woke, to find the wind roaring. But the glow was still there.

I ran upstairs to the light, fearing that the place had somehow caught fire. It was still alight, but dimmer than it had been: the boat would need to get here soon. I polished the mirrors which reflected the light, cleaning them of soot. When I next looked at the clock, it was eight thirty in the morning, but the sky outside was still dark. The glow inside the lighthouse had faded. I felt a sinking sensation within me: this late, and this dark, signalled dreadful weather. I did not go out at all that day, but stayed within, nursing the light and trying to stay awake. Had it not been for the clock, I would have lost track of time.

Taking the lamp, I went out onto the island. The darkness must be cloud, but it felt different, stranger, than that. I could not see any stars and there was no light along the horizon. I had never known it so dark. The lamp cast a tiny pool of light ahead of me, but I did not go far, not wanting to fall over the cliff or, indeed, break my ankle in one of the many rabbit burrows that formed a dangerous maze beneath the crust of the island. As I made my way back, the lamp cast light on a lump in the path. At first, I thought it was a stone, but then I realised it was the petrel. Battered by the wind, it must have become exhausted and unable to fly. It lay gasping on the path. I picked it up and carried it back in the pocket of my waterproof, and when we reached the door, I took it inside, into the lighthouse itself rather than my living accommodation beside it.

It was not the first time I had rescued a seabird. Some of them, mainly broken-winged, died, but others had not and I had known the satisfaction of throwing a living bird up into the wild air and watching it soar over the waves. I gave the petrel bread and dried fish. It settled into its box, watching me with a wary dark eye.

I tended the light and in the morning, the petrel was still alive, though it showed no sign of moving. I divided my time between the bird and the light, which seemed to be growing fainter, eaten by the outside dark. There was no sign of the ghost. By this time, I had convinced myself, gloomily, that I had imagined the whole thing.

A night later, the light went out altogether. The boat had still not come. I could hear the sea lashing the rocks and the howl of the wind, but I couldn't do anything. There was no more coal. I had oil for my little lamp, but even with the mirrors it was not enough to warn a ship away. And it was so dark outside, much blacker than it should have been: when I checked the clock, it told me that it was only three in the afternoon. I thought that if I took the lamp outside, I might be able to make my way to the cliff edge: if anyone was nearing the island, they might see the lamp, not so occluded by the glass of the light. When I went downstairs, I had to wrench the door open and the wind snatched it from my hand and slammed it shut. I stumbled to the cliff. Above me, I realised with unease, that I could see the stars, the clouds had gone, but it was still only mid-afternoon. The clock must be wrong, but I could not now remember when I'd last seen the dawn.

And I thought I could see something out to sea, a bobbing light. If it was the coal boat – *any* craft - there would be nothing to warn it away from the rocks. I held the lamp high, trying to see. I thought I could hear voices, but the wind was raging and I was not sure. I waved the lamp, but the shadow in the waves came onwards. As it came closer, my eyes adjusted to the blackness and I saw that it was the coal boat, at last, too late. I shouted; they could not, of course, hear me. Then a shadow shifted in the corner of my vision and I turned to see the ghost. She clutched her shawl about her, but her hair did not move in the wind.

'You have to let me out,' she said.

'What–?'

'Out of the *lighthouse*.' She might as well have rolled her eyes.

'But you're here, with me,' I said.

'My body is in the lighthouse. I'm the bird.'

I thought I had gone quite mad. But I ran with her to the door, and up the stone stairs, and all the way to the room where the light was dark and the petrel rested in its box.

'It's nearly too late,' the ghost said. 'Break the glass!'

She pointed to the window.

'I –'

'Break it! Let me do my work.'

I seized a shovel and beat at the window: a pane shattered under my blow. The bird sprang from its box and flew like an arrow through the tiny diamond gap. Light streamed out in its wake, first the light itself, restored, then a pathway across the sea and spreading, illuminating all the darkness with gold until the sun appeared, going down into a molten ocean. I saw the boat wrench around, missing the point and disappearing behind the cliffs.

'Thank you,' the ghost said behind me.

I turned. She was very shadowy. I could see the wall through her body.

'Who were you?'

'I'm sorry? Oh,' she said, understanding. 'No, I'm not a ghost. I'm a spirit, I suppose you'd call me, but it's a bit old fashioned. I think of myself as an engineer. I make twilight happen. My sister does dawn. Sometimes we swap. But sometimes it gets a bit much and I need a rest. She's supposed to take over when that happens but she doesn't always and she's sulking now. That's why the sun hasn't come up; why I've had to call it. Sister and I don't get along,' she confided. She glanced at the clock. 'Four in the afternoon. Not too bad for a winter's evening. Don't worry. I'll soon get it back on track.' She started to fade.

'Wait!' I cried, but she was already going, dissolving in the golden light, which flooded into the room as the coal boat came back around, to keep me lit for another few weeks. I was, for once, strangely sure of what I had seen. But that night, just in case, I wrote a long letter to the inspector, and asked him to reserve a bed.

Portrait of Tanith Lee by Kathleen Jennings, 2013

Queen of Night

Cecilia Dart-Thornton

Who walks there, by the ruined wall?
She is the Moon, the Queen of Night.
Empress of dreams, with dreams in thrall,
Clouds for her hair, electrum-bright.

Who steals there, in the mythic wood?
She is the Sorceress of Prose
Perhaps a passing while she stood
And plucked one bloom; a crimson rose.

Perhaps a passing while she strayed
And gazed upon the mirror lake
And while she poised there unafraid,
The wolves came down, their thirst to slake.

They lie beneath her jewelled hand,
Tame nightingales attend her words.
This, her estate, her mind-wrought land
And these her subjects, beasts and birds.
Perhaps- a passing while she stroll'd
To dance upon the flowery sward
While sunset stained the sky with gold
And colours of a treasure hoard.
Fair Lady of the Potent Word

Makes brush and pen at one with sword.
She who pierces with the pen
The hearts and souls and minds of Men,
Bewitching as Eurydice
And fey as cats;
that's
Tanith Lee.

About the Contributors

Storm Constantine

Storm is the creator of the *Wraeththu Mythos*, the first trilogy of which was published in the 1980s. Storm is the founder of Immanion Press, created initially to publish her out-of-print back catalogue, but which evolved into the thriving venture it is today. She has written over thirty books, including full length novels, (including *Hermetech* and *Burying the Shadow)*, novellas, short story collections and non-fiction titles, such as *Sekhem Heka*. Her interests include magic and spirituality, Reiki, movies, music and MMOs. Among her many occupations, most of which are unpaid, she runs a Reiki school and a guild called Equilibrium on the EU servers of World of Warcraft. She lives in the Midlands of the UK with her husband and four cats.

Cecilia Dart-Thornton

Cecilia is the author of numerous bestselling fantasy novels, notably the Bitterbynde Trilogy, whose first volume *The Ill-Made Mute* was listed on Amazon's Best, Locus Magazine's Best First Novels and the Sydney Morning Herald's 'Top Twenty'. It is published in five languages and distributed in more than fifty countries around the world.. The daughter of an architect and an academic, she holds a university Arts degree and

a Diploma of Education. Having started out as a schoolteacher she became a full-time writer in 2000. She is a strong supporter of animal rights and her interests include music, the fine arts (particularly Pre-Raphaelite paintings) and edible gardening.

Vera Nazarian

Vera is a two-time Nebula Award Nominee, award-winning artist, and member of Science Fiction and Fantasy Writers of America, a writer with a penchant for moral fables and stories of intense wonder, true love, and intricacy. She is the author of critically acclaimed novels *Dreams of the Compass Rose* and *Lords of Rainbow*, the outrageous parodies *Mansfield Park and Mummies* and *Northanger Abbey and Angels and Dragons* and most recently, *Pride and Platypus: Mr Darcy's Dreadful Secret* in her humorous and surprisingly romantic Supernatural Jane Austen Series, as well as the Renaissance epic fantasy trilogy *Cobweb Bride*, and the high-octane adventure Young Adult dystopian apocalyptic science fiction series *The Atlantis Grail*. After many years in Los Angeles, Vera lives in a small town in Vermont, and uses her Armenian sense of humour and her Russian sense of suffering to bake conflicted pirozhki and make art. Her official author website is www.veranazarian.com

Sarah Singleton

Sarah is the author of the contemporary fantasy novel *The Crow Maiden* and of eight young adult novels, including *Century*, *Heretic* and *The Amethyst Child*, all published by Simon & Schuster UK. Century won the Booktrust Teen Award and the Children of the Night Award for best gothic novel in 2005. Her short stories have been published in a variety of magazines and anthologies including Interzone, Black Static, Timepieces and Nemonymous. Sarah has worked as a journalist and a creative writing teacher, and she is currently an English teacher at a Wiltshire comprehensive school.

Kari Sperring

Kari Sperring grew up dreaming of joining the musketeers and saving France, only to discover that the company had been disbanded in 1776. Disappointed, she became a historian instead and as Kari Maund has written and published five books and many articles on Celtic and Viking history: Her first novel *Living with Ghosts* was published by DAW books in March 2009: her second, *The Grass King's Concubine*, came out, also from DAW, in August 2012. She lives in Cambridge, England, with her partner Phil and two very determined cats, who guarantee that everything she writes will have been thoroughly sat upon. She's currently at work on her third and fourth novels at once, because she needs more complications in her life. She can be found at http://www.karisperring.com, on Facebook (Kari Sperring), Twitter (@karisperring) and on Live Journal as la_marquise_de_.

Sam Stone

Sam Stone began writing aged 11 after reading her first adult fiction book, *The Collector* by John Fowles. Sam's writing has appeared in many anthologies of poetry and prose. Her first novel, *Killing Kiss*, was the fulfilment of a lifelong dream, and won the Silver Award for Best Horror Novel in *ForeWord Magazine*'s book of the year awards in 2007. The sequels, *Futile Flame* and *Demon Dance* went on to become finalists in the same awards for 2009/2010 and were shortlisted for

The British Fantasy Society Awards for Best Novel. Sam also won Best Short Fiction for her story 'Fool's Gold' which first appeared in the NewCon Press Anthology *The Bitten Word*. Other short stories have appeared in a variety of anthologies. Sam's website is at www.sam-stone.com, and she can be found on Twitter as @samstonereal.

Freda Warrington

Freda Warrington is the author of 21 fantasy novels. She started writing as soon as she could hold a pen, and in her teens she was inspired by visionary writers, especially Tanith Lee. Her first novel, *A Blackbird in Silver*, appeared in 1986. Her works include *A Taste of Blood Wine* (a gothic vampire romance set in the 1920s), *Dracula the Undead* (award-winning 1997 sequel to Bram Stoker's classic novel), *The Amber Citadel* (epic fantasy) and *Elfland* (contemporary fantasy, winner of the Romantic Times Best Fantasy Novel Award). Born and raised in rural Leicestershire, Freda has a long-standing interest in that most fascinating of kings, Richard III. Her 2003 novel *The Court of the Midnight King: a Dream of Richard III* was recently reissued in print and ebook form to celebrate the re-interment of the king's remains. To learn more, please visit her website, www.fredawarrington.com.

Liz Williams

Liz Williams is a science fiction and fantasy writer living in Glastonbury, England, where she is co-director of a witchcraft supply business. She is currently published by Bantam Spectra (US) and Tor Macmillan (UK), also Night Shade Press and appears regularly in *Realms of Fantasy*, *Asimov's* and other magazines. She is the secretary of the Milford SF Writers' Workshop, and also teaches creative writing and the history of Science Fiction. Her novels include

The Ghost Sister, *Winterstrike*, and *Worldsoul*. She has also had two short story collections published, and her third, *The Light Warden* will appear from NewCon Press this year. Her novel *Banner of Souls* has been nominated for the Philip K Dick Memorial Award, along with three previous novels, and the Arthur C Clarke Award. Liz writes a CIF column for the Guardian and reviews for SFX.

Tanith Lee Books
Published by Immanion Press

The Colouring Books Series

Greyglass
To Indigo
L'Amber
Killing Violets
Ivoria
Cruel Pink
*Turquoiselle

Animate Objects
(limited edition short story collection now out of print)

*Ghosteria 1: The Stories
*Ghosteria 2: The Novel: Zircons May be Mistaken

*A Different City
(three novellas)

*Legenda Maris
(short story collection)

*also available in eBook through Kindle

IMMANION PRESS
Purveyors of Speculative Fiction

Legenda Maris by Tanith Lee

The sea... restless, eerie, all-powerful and mysterious – occasionally she reveals her secrets.

Legenda Maris comprises eleven tales of the ocean and her denizens, including two that are original to this collection – 'Leviathan' and 'Land's End, The Edge of The Sea' – which were among the last stories Tanith Lee wrote. In this treasure chest of tales, the author works her beguiling, linguistic sorcery to conjure mermaids who are as deadly as they are lovely, the hidden coves of lonely fishing villages harbouring mysteries, and fantastical ships that haunt the waves. She explores the relationship between the sea and the land, and the occasional meetings between those who dwell above and below the waters – meetings that are sometimes wondrous and sometimes fatal, often both. Papaperback. ISBN: 978-1-907737-67-1 £11.99, $17.99

The Moonshawl by Storm Constantine

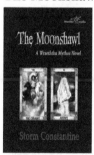

Ysbryd drwg... the bad ghost. Hired by Wyva, the phylarch of the Wyvachi tribe, Ysobi goes to Gwyllion to create a spiritual system based upon local folklore, but soon discovers some of that folklore is out of bounds, taboo... Secrets lurk in the soil of Gwyllion, and the old house Meadow Mynd. The fields are soaked in blood and echo with the cries of those who were slaughtered there, almost a century ago. Old hatreds and a thirst for vengeance have been awoken by the approaching coming of age of Wvya's son, Myvyen. If the harling is to survive, Ysobi must lay the ghosts to rest and scour the tainted soil of malice. But the *ysbryd drwg* is strong, built of a century of resentment and evil thoughts. Is it too powerful, even for a scholarly hienama with Ysobi's experience and skill? *The Moonshawl* is a standalone supernatural story, set in the world of Storm Constantine's ground-breaking, science fantasy Wraeththu mythos. Paperback. ISBN: 978-1-907737-62-6 £11.99, $20.99

Immanion Press
http://www.immanion-press.com
info@immanion-press.com

NEWCON PRESS

http://newconpress.co.uk/

The very best in fantasy, science fiction, and horror

Colder Greyer Stones by Tanith Lee

Released to commemorate the author being honoured with a Lifetime Achievement Award at the 2013 World Fantasy Convention, this stunning collection of stories provides further evidence of why Tanith Lee is held in such high regard by fans and contemporaries alike. The book features twelve wonderful, rich-textured tales including the brand new novelette "The Frost Watcher" and five stories previously available only in the (sold out) signed limited edition "Cold Grey Stones".
Paperback: ISBN 978-1-907069-60-4   £9.99

The Light Warden by Liz Williams

Liz Williams possesses the mind of a scientist and the soul of a pagan; her words paint the world in eldritch shades, revealing the familiar in subtly altered forms that make us question our own understanding. In 2010, NewCon Press released Liz's last collection, the critically acclaimed *A Glass of Shadow*, and we are now proud to release her next, *The Light Warden*, volume 11 in the Imaginings series.

Fifteen stories, two of which were selected for *Year's Best* anthologies and seven that are original to this collection. *The Light Warden* showcases Liz Williams at her best.
ISBN: 978-1-910935-01-9
Limited edition hardback £22.99

LEAVES of GOLD PRESS

Leaves of Gold Press publishes fantasy novels, children's books, and well-loved classic fiction.

TANITH LEE

PHANTASYA

Phantasya is a collection of nineteen splendid Tanith Lee tales, hand-picked by the author. These extraordinary journeys into Lee's hugely popular fantasy worlds span 31 years of her extraordinary writing career and include four never-before-published stories: 'Clouden', 'Book Cover', 'Jade-Eye' and 'Questorday'. The tales in this anthology, saturated with magical color and light, have been compared to the writings of William Morris or Lord Dunsany. Sometimes disturbing, always beguiling, they will spirit readers into imaginary realms like no others.

CONTENTS: Black As A Rose, Book Cover, Clouden, Deux Amours D'Une Sorcière, Flowers For Faces, Thorns For Feet, Foolish, Wicked, Clever and Kind, The Girl Who Lost Her Looks, Jade-Eye, The Lancastrian Blush, Mirage and Magia, Odds Against the Gods, The One We Were, The Pale Girl, the Dark Mage and the Green Sea, Questorday, Sleeping Tiger, The Tale of the Tailor's Tail, White As Sin, Now, The Witch of the Moon, Zinder.
ISBN: 978-1-925110-56-2, paperback, $29.95

Visit our web site to view our full catalogue, including titles by Cecilia Dart-Thornton:

http://www.leavesofgoldpress.com/

NOW AVAILABLE

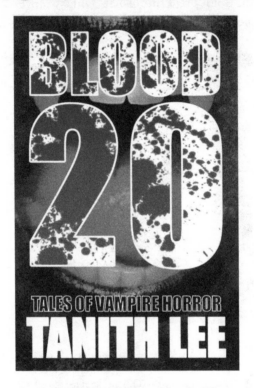

Available in an exclusive signed edition
only from www.telos.co.uk
ISBN: 978-1-84583-909-3

Coming in 2016 from Telos Publishing:

TANITH LEE: A TO Z
26 previously uncollected tales of fantasy and horror

Printed in the USA
CPSIA information can be obtained
at www.ICGtesting.com
LVHW030226100923
757647LV00068B/702